IVORY'S STORY

IVORY'S STORY

Eugen Bacon

NEWCON
PRESS

NewCon Press
England

First published in the UK, December 2020 by
NewCon Press
41 Wheatsheaf Road,
Alconbury Weston,
Cambs, PE28 4LF

NCP251 (limited edition hardback)
NCP252 (paperback)

10 9 8 7 6 5 4 3 2 1

ISBN:

978-1-912950-76-8 (hardback)
978-1-912950-77-5 (paperback)

Cover art by Vincent Sammy
Cover layout by Ian Whates

Typesetting and editorial meddling by Ian Whates
Book layout by Ian Whates

Dedication:

For the stories we yearn to tell, the diversity of our voices.
    I am black.
        I am 'other'.
            I am many.

Betwixt. A sum of cultures.
There are multiple points of intersection in blackness – I dedicate this story to my duality as an African Australian. Where does one culture begin, where does it end?

To all within and without cultural borderlands in modern cities. Same, same but different – our humanity that pervades the everyday.

To the river of my clan
your waters nourish the cabbage palm and mandisa pine
that feed my people.

To the mountain of my people
your peaks sentry the plains from menace
that lusts for my spirit.

To the rock of my spirit
your minerals replenish me from dust
that sweeps over my history.

One: The Scientist

Pearly stars mottled a black sky in Gorge precinct. A slice of moon cast its glow on a crag streaked copper, and the hue spread to the flora neighbouring a permanent water hole. A few feet away, an astrophysicist on retreat from stellar quests rested along the levy bank of the small country town. Dusk carried scents of native hibiscus and wild passion fruit plant that infused the atmosphere. Sporadic coolabah trees, so twisted they resembled phantom snakes, coiled along the jagged cliff with spikes of spinifex in between.

The scientist was relaxed in this effort, her study of virgin wilderness in sultry country at the outskirts of Stone Town a well-rewarded pastime. Earlier in the day she had tested primitive time keeping. Using measure of hours by fingers at eye-level to separate the base of the sun from the horizon, she had proven the hypothesis of native talent on matters of natural phenomena. In the isolation of pure beauty, nirvana of rugged terrain speckled with herbs and creatures, she had found in wide spectrum a few things about dawn, sunset and twilight. She understood how a study of flora or fauna, and the way it behaved – for example catching the timbre in the song of a dusky grasswren's song, or calculating the angle of a bush tomato's petal, aligned with the native precision of timekeeping. Now she bent and shone her torch towards the ground. With a free hand, she fingered cold rock.

Further north, an assembly of stars illuminated an escarpment. A narrow footpath along the cliffs led her into a remote shelter. Inside, using her torch, she found rock art. Her face flushed with the discovery of a primitive art gallery. She felt like James Cook. Gently her palms stroked a tongue-flicking goanna lizard, solid in sacred stone. She followed drawings outside the sanctuary and, at the base of a separate cave wall past a dark monolith north, she found a red kangaroo nurturing a Joey in a pouch.

She imagined herself giving a lecture to animated students back home. 'Each animal embodied fundamental belief, ancestry and life in a symbolic harmony of man and animal.' She laughed out loud, awash with exhilaration. Her find was a mosaic of legend, tradition and religion carved on rock, a limitless interdependence of spirit and land in an ancient way of life.

She traced the height and grace of a family of emus. More spirit people in headdress. The rest of the phallic rocks were bare, eroded. An array of spiked banksias spread branches with orange flowers above the crag.

Instinct more than anything else drew her gaze skyward. A soft whistle escaped her lips. She shrugged off her rucksack, pulled a travel telescope from it. Quickly she unfolded its legs and trained it – not on scatters of immobile sparkles in the heavens but on one unusual star tumbling in the sky, a star iridescent even with unaided eye. Before she could manage one still shot it fired into space, cutting miles, miles… and vanished.

She sat on hallowed ground unaware of the violation her unwarranted presence caused. She ran mental calculations of the moon and its angle and range relative to the current date. She estimated the speed and burning of the meteorite she had witnessed. She even jogged a few miles in hope of finding debris: stone or metal. Anything indicative of a meteor shower that confirmed a shooting star.

She found nothing.

She returned to her B&B in the heart of Stone Town with elation. Next morning, she scanned all major papers for news of sightings or a sonic boom. Nothing. Disillusioned, she dismissed the fireball as an anomalous star whose glow gave the impression of speed and tail. All that glory... It was nothing more than a stupid star.

Two: A History

1.

Izett was five, Sister Immaculata was… who knew how old? She looked young, sounded young, compared to Sister Hildegarde the mother superior.

Sister Immaculata had a rosebud mouth, sang like a lark. She was gentler than a dove. Best of all, she told stories. And Izett loved stories. They were tales from the Bible, pretty much all of them. Sister Immaculata blossomed in her retelling of each story. Like the one of Jonah who fled having to preach to the naughty people of Nineveh, and got himself swallowed by a whale.

'Why aren't there girl heroes in the Bible?' asked Izett.

'There are girl heroes everywhere.'

'Like where?'

'Right here. You're a hero. A real fire cracker.'

'But I'm not in the Bible.'

'The Bible was written by a bunch of men, each with a theology.'

'What's a tho-ology?'

'Early thinking as far as I'm concerned. It has refined over time, but still contains all the notions of men who thought they knew everything.'

The idea of priests with their cunning and theology put frost in Izett's heart. They were a danger to anyone who didn't argue or fight with them. She shivered as she considered the many definitions of creation she'd read, heard or imagined, the twists and tonics of each sacred verse. The secrets, many secrets, mostly imagined. Peering with reluctance through the inner ice, she understood that she was freezing from the concept of super saver priests and their grateful harvest of believers, all who always, always had time for communion. Tick. Tock.

She looked at Sister Immaculata. 'Do you know everything?'

Sister Immaculata went all pensive. They were sat on the third-bottom step to the library from the outdoors, feet aground. She took Izett's hand, looked out yonder at the great big fence that locked them inside the compound.

'You're the most fortunate of all children here.'

'You don't know anything.'

'Families want you.'

'No, they don't.'

'Try to stay in the houses they take you.'

'I like it here.'

'But it's...' Sister Immaculata shrugged. 'It's St Vincent's. You know. Sister Hildegarde and all that. She doesn't mean to be harsh.'

Izett looked at the welts fresh still on her little legs.

Sister Hildegarde was cunning as a crow near sandwiches at a picnic. Izett remembered one such crow, its beady eye and greyed beak. Its black, black feathers shiny as oil. It was a sunny day. She had lost count of foster mums, and this one was trying really hard with her butter and kaya sandwiches. Izett swallowed each triangled bite size in a mouthful, as the foster mum – was her name Etsy? – with her straight straw hair, stockinged legs curled beneath her skirt carpeting the grass, nodded with much

5

optimism and a smile. They had a moment right there, just Izett wasn't sure what was making the moment. She was trying to make this work but could only think of Sister Immaculata's absence in the moment. She reached for another sandwich, gobbled the rich texture of coconut jam swollen with palm sugar and condensed milk. That's when she saw the crow. It ambled up, stared her in the eye like a weaponed bandit. So mesmerised was Izett by the crow's boldness, she didn't move as it dipped its beak and drew a triangle of sandwich, whole, from her hand. It did not fly away, simply stepped off right and took a stand. It ate the sandwich, peck after peck, until it was satisfied. It abandoned the torn sandwich and its scattered innards. Izett was still watching in quiet shock at the audacity of the bird when it hopped two steps, flapped its wings, and flew away with a caw, but not before a parting look of complete disdain. At what? wondered Izett.

With boldness matching the crow Sister Hildegarde cashed in on the children through government funding and private charities, dipped her beak, peck after peck. But she didn't appear to do much to cherish the children who were her investments, who would remain scattered innards when she was done with them.

'Why can't you just try?' asked Sister Immaculata.

Izett looked around the gated mansion that kept secret its bathrooms and kitchens and fireplaces – only visible when you cleaned them – while the children, all name-tagged, slept in stables refitted into boarding rooms. The compound in a progressive part of Sydney did not have lush green lawns like the ones she'd seen in some foster homes. This honeycomb mansion had no space for play, but it was full of corridors to scrub.

Dead leaves, that's what lurked inside. Cracked leaves, crushable to fragments blowing like dirt in the wind. It was a matter of light, what angle shadows took. The leaves entered her core. She tried to remember all the things that made her feel, things like the prick of a thorn on tender heels. The sting of a whip on soft skin. The taste of chalk – its crumble on the tongue. The tinkle of a bell as a bicycle she'd never ride whooshed past. The sight of birds in surreal formation on a clear horizon out yonder. The swarm of insects like sombre raindrops to some place not here…

She closed her eyes, willed for feeling. But there was nothing to feel, just the dead leaves rising and falling, passing without name tags or beliefs in a space between black clouds.

'This is not a proper home for you,' said Sister Immaculata.

'It is!' The dead leaves and their dust whirled and whirled and imploded suddenly and completely with a force that thrust Izett to her feet. 'It is!' She ran, and the leaves whizzed away with her. 'A hundred times it is!'

2.

Not all foster homes were bad.

Like the one that had Emma, the nine-year-old with the blood sickness, something about her marrow. She was thin and frail, but she was kind.

Emma and Sister Immaculata were each an ancient soul trapped in a frail human body. The first time Izett saw Emma, all she saw was a halo and a shadow on sticks.

'Why are you walking on sticks?'

'They're not sticks, stupid. They're crutches.'

'Why do you need them?'

'How old are you?' Emma answered her with a question.

'Five. Maybe six.'

'Why do they call you Izett? It's a stupid name.'

'You can call me Ivory.'

'What's that on your neck?'

'My mother gave me. Actually – I came with it. It was her only possession.'

'Can I touch it?'

'It burns… people.'

'Like who?'

'Some bad boys where I stayed. They tried to take it but it burnt their hands.'

'Let me.' Emma hobbled and fell at Ivory. She fumbled for the amulet. It glowed at her touch. 'You sure it burns people?'

'I guess it likes you.'

'Come. I'll show you something.'

Emma hobbled with her crutches from the lounge and crashed into a cupboard on the corridor. It was heaven. It was full of toys – Ivory had never seen so many toys. She liked Mr Egg, Big Teddy and Dotti the Elephant.

But mostly she played alone because Emma was always sick. If she wasn't on crutches, she was in a wheelchair or lying in bed. She was a soul, there wasn't much to her body. It was so broken, the body, it was useless to pay attention to it. Each day the body faded, Emma's soul radiated brighter. Her kindness never ebbed.

Even when the sickness took her to hospital and she stayed there for a week. She came back the colour of a ghost, unable to use her legs, bedridden. Ivory peered through the window from outside, she was still peering long after the preoccupied foster mum left.

Emma turned her head, beckoned with a weak finger. Ivory entered the room and its sharp smell of scouring detergent. Emma pointed at a chest of drawers near the bed.

'Open the second one.' Her voice was a croak and a whisper.

Ivory pulled out a solid rectangle wrapped in gold foil. 'What's this?'

'I was brave with the needle.'

'Where?'

'Up my spine.'

'Show me.'

'It hurts to move.'

Ivory went to return the foil and its treasure into the drawer. 'Take it. It's yours,' murmured Emma.

It was a bar of chocolate. Ivory had never eaten anything like it before. The first bite, a melting taste, it filled her mouth with a warmth that was rich with butter and nut, and a hint of soil as she swallowed. She squirrelled the rest of the bar, only took a nibble when she was sad.

The foster mum was a tall wiry thing with worried eyes, always fretting, much distracted. She gave Ivory food or medicine or a hug when it was due. But she was overwhelmed with nursing and chores, she never had time for much else.

The foster dad, he was okay… He offered to push her on the swing one day and was astonished when she shuddered, leapt from the swing and crawled to hide inside the dog house. Later, at dinner, she remembered how he looked at her. It was with disappointment and something like compassion. His was the kind of look you gave a broken kitten that snarled and spat and clawed – it wouldn't let you pet it, even as it breathed its last.

Later Emma got sicker and Ivory cut a square of her hidden chocolate. She offered a piece first to the foster mum, then to the foster dad. He started to shake his head, then he took the broken piece and began to cry. Big manly sobs that sounded like the kick of a wrecked engine.

Ivory put Dotti the elephant into his hands and piped, 'She wants a cuddle,' as he cried.

And then Emma was too sick for Ivory to be present, and she found herself back in the system hugging the little elephant that had seen a grown man cry.

3.

She was fifteen, he was eighteen.

He was one boy she nearly trusted to become a boyfriend. He was a sandgroper from Perth. Benni.

She met him at a pub, he lasted a night and a day.

Benni was a bleach-haired, blue-eyed good looker with the bronze sheen you get from a spray can – just his was from the sun.

'You're a ripper,' he said. 'A real bloody beauty.'

But he wasn't keen on getting into her undies first off. Perhaps that's what gave them this connection, like when he talked about where he grew up.

'Blue and yellow,' he said. 'The colours of Perth. The sand is bloody hot, I say. You just ditch your towel and hop, hop, hop across the sizzle to the water. You don't know how the sand is hot.'

'And you swam?'

'Right there in the Indian Ocean. Next stop Africa or India.'

'Really?'

He laughed. 'Never got that far. But you could swim all the way to the pylon. Sometimes waves smashed at your face, but you could swim them. Then you shimmied up the rope and you jumped off it and you became a kid in the water.'

She imagined over and over the thrill. The exhilaration of sprinting on yellow sand as it burnt your bare feet. Swimming naked against giant blue waves as they smashed at your face. Scooting up the tall, green and black pylon as it hugged your nakedness. Releasing the rope under a fierce burning sun and slapping feet first into the ocean as it roared.

She lived in a hostel, he at the YMCA. The best strategy was to arrange to meet the next evening at the botanical garden, which they did. He rocked up with a bottle of rum, some cheap shit manufactured in a sewer. She looked at him in his sunburnt beauty, and it didn't matter what shit came out of that bottle. He laughed, and the rum tasted like nectar. All went well until they got drunk, so pissed they walked zigzag and they knew it.

It was closing time. They were giggling about something, about being locked in for the night in the garden, then he made his move. It was the way he did it: perhaps it was the grope of his palm on her buttock, or the leer of his smile on his drunken face. And even though Benni was just a boy his act resurrected something, and all she saw was a foster dad after foster dad she'd run away from.

She smashed him across the fence with her whole body and a fist.

4.

It was a basement club named *Cherry*, a seedy joint.

There was a man at the bar, another good looker, nicely built, his voice was full of sand and there was depth in his eye.

She looked from him to catch the waiter's attention, and that was when the man at the bar spoke.

'Come here often?'

She took time before she looked at him. 'That's a bit jaded.'

'You're a hard catch.' He smiled. 'Let me practise on you.'

'Move along,' she said.

'Buy you a martini?'

'I'm a soda and rum kind of girl.'

'Get you one.'

'I'm with friends,' she said.

The waiter was a soft type with chestnut eyes, now he faced her across the counter. 'What shall we get you?'

'An espresso martini,' she said, and didn't look at the man at the bar as she paid.

It was 8pm. The main act was meant to start, but there was no sign of the band or the lead singer. A DJ was doing his thing, and it was random. People dotted the dance floor.

Before she could blink, it was jam packed, but that was two and a half espresso martinis later, vodka and coffee swirling in her head. The nutty bitterness mellowed her with its pleasant kick.

The secondary act was mediocre, a young girl who ate up the microphone. There were bodies on the floor everywhere, and Ivory was caught in the crush.

Suddenly she needed air.

She squeezed past the horde, stumbled out of the basement club.

'What happened to your friends?' A sandy voice.

She turned to give him a chance but caught his gaze.

It reminded her of the way one dad at a foster home looked at her before she bit him, before they sent her away with all her belongings in a garbage bag, before she got to know his surname and hope that one day it might be hers. All she carried in the plastic bag were two old dresses, a tiny framed photo of herself in a bassinet as a baby – smoky green eyes big as a dolly's, her tattered rag dolly named Janey, her jungle pyjamas and a toothbrush. The look the foster dad gave her, same look that the man at the bar gave her, it was a Lion King look. Not the regal one like Mufasa's discernment look but the crooked one like Scar's gobbler look. Like she was free meat and he was starving.

So when the man said, 'What happened to your friends?' and gave her that look, she pulled her hand and whipped his face in a backhand that made him stagger, more from astonishment.

'Jesus!' He spat on the ground, like the foster dad did as her cab pulled away to take her back to the system.

Self-loathing like an engulfing mouth swallowed her whole and she sat on the curb as ebony horses stamped the road, or were they pounding in her head? She opened her eyes and lone cars winked their headlights, whooshed past in search of daylight and a clean start. Some blinked left and turned, or right and turned, at the junction with its traffic lights that went red the colour of rage, amber the colour of indifference, green the colour of lonesomeness and there were more reds than greens, a few ambers in between. She put her head in her arms and cried her flood river that raced into a mercury sea.

5.

'What's this?' said a man's voice.

She lifted her head through her tears. It was not the motherfucker from the basement club.

The new man was looking down at her and in his hand he held a briefcase. 'Take a hike,' she hiccupped through scarlet lipstick.

He was a cross between a geek and a feral, a man with unruly curls doused with pitch-black tar. He tried to raise her by the hand from the curb stone, the place he found her at minutes after midnight and she was holding her head in her hands, and sobbing tears that rivered down her face to soak her snazzy little outfit that accentuated her adolescence.

'It was darkness and bare land in the ancient night,' he said. He ignored her incredulous gaze and went on with his rambling. 'This is the story of how the sun woman met the spirit of the moon and he looked at her with big eyes and a halo –'

'Keep walking, mate,' she recovered enough to say.

'And the spirit of the moon said, *Come.*' He stretched out a hand and waited for her to take it. She slapped it away. 'Together, the sun woman and the spirit of the moon travelled across the earth and over the seas –'

'Think this is fucking Timbuktu?'

He shifted his briefcase. 'Timbuktu's an ancient city in what is now Mali, north of the Niger River.'

'A fucking academic. What's your name then – Willie or is it Sweet Cheeks?'

'You can call me Bahati.'

'Nice name. Now drop the fucking bag and I'll biff you on the spot.'

'It's not a bag, it's a compendium.'

'I wouldn't give a toss if it was Pandora's box.'

'You are unlikely to find it here, Pandora's box. It was an artefact in Greek mythology, a story of why things happen, and it had everything to do with Zeus, Prometheus, and his brother Epimetheus, and nothing to do with us.'

'Fuck off.'

13

'Principally, intercourse is an *in*, an act of insertion, not an *off*.'

'Will you just get over yourself?'

He fingered the amulet on her neck. It flashed a play of colour at his touch, bright orange and then red and then black.

'It doesn't burn?' she asked, astonished.

'An opal is formed from rain,' he said. 'When water seeps down a rock, the silica it creates hardens and forms the gemstone.'

'Good to know.'

'Ancient mythology assigns prophetic powers to the opal, some stories giving its origin to Zeus' tears of joy when they beat the Titans.'

'Do you ever stop?'

'Academising? Never. Let's go for a beach walk,' he said. 'I think of life as a seagull walking barefoot on sand, connected to the soil. It's the greatest earthing. You look out across the choppy waves, kite surfers soaring on wind –'

'At this time of the night? I don't think so.'

'Just stay with the seagull, hopping along a frothy wash, flapping its white wings. The beach – the greatest earthing. It's good for you. It's good for anyone who wears a beautiful stone formed by rain.'

Her laugh was meant to be sarcastic. 'I don't know what you've been drinking.'

'Ever drank a Malbec paired with cheese?'

'What?'

6.

He put down his briefcase, knelt beside her and tried to put calming hands on her shoulder. But she pounded his chest with fists, pounded until her own hands hurt, then she whipped him with words, obscenities that clung, insults so personal they struck barbs. 'You couldn't put it straight if I gave it to you for free. Get a dog up ya.'

It was an unfair fight against this mild-mannered man who was no imposing motherfucker, not like the man who had left her sitting on the curb and bawling her eyes out. But she was used to lashing at men with words, slaps and kicks, and some fights she won, some she lost. Now she was sparring in the ring, bouncing and bracing to administer a knock-out or die trying, but this man cornered her at the ropes with his philosophy.

Turned out what should have been a bloodbath was nothing but a tantrum, and she burst into fresh tears. He sat beside her on the curb and looked at his hands as he spoke. They were soft and clean hands, immaculate fingers whose nails were clipped.

'Back home we go to wilderness country in a plant-hunting ceremony, dancing and chanting and calling out to the mandisa pine to give up her cones. Now what you need to know is that mandisa cones are tough things to find, they hide inside the height of a tree and the tree helps to conceal each cone by wrapping it up in her foliage. And even though the cones are big like watermelons, and you might see them up high, they weigh as much as bowling balls and there is a skill to harvesting them.'

He cast her a glance and his eyes reminded her of the eyes of a koala she once saw in a zoo, dark coloured buttons with something dreamy in them, and the keeper had told her the animal was about to go to sleep.

Now spent from fury, silenced with a story – she loved stories – she listened to the mild-mannered man. He was wearing pale shorts. She noticed for the first time the tone of his skin, salt brown head to toe, and his legs stretched out on the cracked curb were thin and long and she thought of a stick insect, and she wondered if he climbed the mandisa pine or used a pole to cajole the cones from nature's steeple.

She could not resist the question. 'Don't cones just fall to the ground when they're ready?'

'Not mandisa cones. The mandisa pine is sentient, fierce as a mum protecting her brood, and she holds tight to every single one of them. She will spit and hump and chase people from her cones, she will hit you with her twigs and leaves. So you must lull her with smoke and song, and then from a distance spear each cone down.'

'That's when you get to eat what's inside?'

'Once you get a cone, it has maybe 70 nuts if you're lucky and each nut is clasped inside a super-tough shell – just like you.' He brushed his gaze on her face. 'When you reach the nut, perhaps with a hammer or a rock or a fire and some garden loppers and the shell cracks in halves, you get your first whiff of the buttery nut and you want to eat it right away. But the skill is patience. The longer you hold off and store the nut – like you can bury it in a hole filled up with mud – and the longer you keep it, the sweeter it gets.'

When his arm went around her shoulder, she let it, and when she sneezed and he offered her his jacket, she took it. Something about him was as welcoming as a fermented nut served up with butter, but it still surprised her when she heard herself say, 'Would you like a drink with me?'

7.

Bahati did not take her to a pub, but to his bachelor pad at the university. It was a self-contained closet no bigger than an isolation cell in a supermax prison. Maybe that was an exaggeration, but the point – to whom exactly Ivory was unsure – was that the cubicle was a tiny walk-in no better than a lean-to. He had all his books on one shelf, most labelled Professor Bahati Moody, and there was one tome titled: *The Mountain, the River and the Emu*. She lifted the title. 'Moody?'

'Yes, a real grouch.'

Next to the shelf was a silver and gold stereo whose two speakers were scattered about the room. One was dangled near the ceiling, and the other plonked on a chest of drawers beside the six-foot long, four-foot wide small double with a fat mattress. He didn't invite her to sit, and there was nowhere to go but the bed or the toilet seat in the bathroom, so she sat on the fat mattress and it held firmly, not sagged.

He boiled the kettle next to the stereo, stirred hot water and some powder from a packet into a mug, whipped in some thick cream from a mini fridge on the floor, handed her the mug of hot chocolate and watched as she drank. He stood by the door, still watching, and between sips she found herself talking without encouragement.

She told him about *Cherry* and the good looker at the bar who ogled her like the ravenous lion Scar might, and spat on the ground like the foster dad did.

'It drowned my self-worth over and over. So I sat on the curb.'

He crossed the room, not much of it to reach her. 'Oh, shit,' he said and kissed her.

She clung to the warmth of his lips, to his tenderness, and then to the current that flowed from his lips to electrify her whole body and float her mind. She closed her eyes, her feet on air.

He pushed her away, not unkindly. She looked at him with bafflement.

'The skill is patience,' almost roughly, and he walked out of the room.

Three: The Curse of Multiples

1.

He was tall as a pine, a beautiful man dark as night. His eyes were onyx.

He lived in the land of the Great Chief Goanna who studied the white man's language and took to wearing his hair in a bob cut. The same Chief Goanna who paid for his education by working in overalls as a cleaner in the big city infirmary of the white man, who was best renowned for returning to his people and bringing greatness to their land. There, in native land, Chief Goanna shaved his head, discarded his overalls, wore bark loin and lifted a club to go to Parliament and save his country with eloquence from the greed of a white settler who wanted to put a mall, a restaurant and a spa in the burial grounds of the forefathers inside the Valley of Dreams.

People spoke of Chief Goanna for generations. Praised him for taking the white man's education and outwitting them with it. He didn't need to open up the sea to make them heed, all he needed was his tongue to command the white man's language.

Now, the man named Muntu did not open up the sea either, nor did he bring heroism to his people. Matter of fact, he was an outcast. He was the third line descendant of a medicine man named Kuntu, the one who opposed the crowning of Chief Duppe – the great grandfather of the current Chief Mezzanine, a small man of shifty eyes who stole yellow-skinned women for his brides from their villages in the dead of night.

And though Muntu's eyes flashed like opals and he looked like a god of thunder, his voice was calm as light rain.

2.

He knew from the start about twins.

And while the people of the land no longer cast new-born identicals at the edge of the forest for the dingo to take, twins still carried ill luck. Despite this knowledge, Muntu loved Dotto. She was one of twins. But Dotto was also the child of the shifty Chief Mezzanine. The day she was born, three breaths behind her twin Kulwa, the witch man pointed his bone to cast out calamity and save the twins from inheriting the varmint nature of their father.

Where Kulwa's eyes took the colour of sunshine, Dotto's sang of diamonds. Where Kulwa's skin was white as goat milk, Dotto's was olive, soft as a riverbed. Where Kulwa's smile reminded of claret orchids, Dotto's laughter bubbled as eager as thought. But for all those claret orchids, the gods favoured riverbed skin, and within two moons Kulwa, the elder by three breaths, breathed her last.

Despite his knowledge of twins, of Dotto's laughter that sucked breath from the lungs of her sibling, Muntu loved. In so doing, he wrote his crime. It made him fugitive, trapped in a love that could never be open outside the secrets of a grass hut.

One night of many nights, the dusk before it happened, Dotto curled against Muntu's skin inside her hut. A soft, blue fall of her hair caressed his chin. A midnight glow from a plump moon stole inward through the thatch. It squeezed through a crack on the mud wall and enriched the olive in the finger that stroked Muntu's ribs.

Diamond eyes sought opal eyes.

'You should not be here.'

'Do you want me to leave?'

'No.'

'But your father –'

'He is not here.' Her fingers roamed.

'Such unnecessary risk: villagers are pouring everywhere. We must stop being foolish.'

The din of festivity filtered through the walls. It was the celebration of Chief Mezzanine's consummation of a brand new marriage: a bride thieved from Saltbush Country.

'Nothing is foolish about loving,' she said. 'Take me away from here.'

'There are no borders to love. We must not spoil it with rash decisions.'

'Without the fool of my father between us, we can find happiness together.'

A big hand cupped her small face. 'Our love could never be stronger. I can be anywhere you are.'

'Arm in arm in the stars?'

'Time will be the shaping of that.'

'Why?' She toyed with the black opal amulet he wore on his neck. His lucky stone, he called it, handed down through generations. It was a stone that liked her – she knew this because it let her touch it.

'*Timing* is important. Do not be saddened by caution.'

'You will worry me out of it.'

He held her as she trembled. He closed his eyes. When he spoke, his voice was torn from his throat. 'Why must we speak sombre things when there is much more to do?'

She kissed his brow, the tip of his nose, the curls on his chest. He opened his eyes.

'Come,' he said. 'Let us sleep.'

'Harlequna!' she exclaimed, eyes wide on a tear-drop face. 'Now you want to sleep?'

'Close your eyes.' He spoke to her hair. 'I want you to think about the sea.'

'I have never seen a sea. How can I think about one?'

'It is giant water that is green, and it is full of waves.'

'Like the waves that Great Chief Goanna parted and the waters swallowed the white man?'

He smiled. 'Like those waters.'

She nestled in the crook of his arm.

'Open your inside eye, that which dwells in your heart. Feel the sea.'

'Going sway, sway?' Her breaths soft and swift like a baby's.

'Pushing. Prodding,' he whispered. 'Like this and this. Ripples, tides going thrust, thrust… And when pressure is too big, when the sea begins to overflow, it rocks, and feeds into another river.'

3.

He woke to a trill at dawn. A bell bird was singing its sunrise song. Dotto slept with the simplicity and abandonment of an infant.

She stirred and touched his back. 'Greetings of dawn.'

'I must teach you to share a bed.'

'You exaggerate.'

He kissed her forehead, started rising from the soft bed of red kangaroo skin but she clutched him, clung to him.

'I must,' he said gently. He touched her face, warm, silent tears on it. He cupped her face. 'Remember to play your music for me.'

'What music?'

'The one of the sea and the night. It does not matter where I am. I will hear it.'

He stepped out of the hut to a whip of early morning breeze on his face. He slipped from hut to hut, clambered a mud wall barrier between guards and fell into a cluster of red Kangaroo Paw.

Dotto's taste lingered on his lips like bush mint. The sweep of her hair soft still on his neck. The roam of her fingers on his chest. Diamond eyes begging him to stay.

4.

Two sleeps, and they seemed like several worlds to him, worlds that separated him from Dotto and her music, a dirge of sea and rain, night and smog, her yen for him spilling from a flute.

Dusk made shadows of the walls that towered arm lengths from the saltbush. Somewhere in the chief's compound, Dotto was warm and waiting for him. When he found her, she would press her lips, soft and trembling, against his. She would guide his fingers to her secret places. She would wrap her legs around his waist, as wisps of baby breaths brushed lightly at the back of his neck.

He slipped from the shrubbery, away from the warm breath of a friendly numbat. He bent low, away from direct view of a guard standing with a long spear on a parapet overlooking the wall. Fingers groped, guiding him blindly. They touched the chief's wall. He felt along hardened mud, found a crack, and then another, and another. He got a grip, pressed his weight against the solid, hoisted himself off the ground and crawled upward.

He paused, swung a leg over the wall, and froze at the snap of a twig. A sentry walked his post and, moments later, there was a rise of laughter along the far gate. Voices rose and dipped in the direction of Chief Mezzanine's hut. A flicker of firelight danced through a wall.

Music rose from the opposite direction. Dotto was playing her flute. She played something light and hollow that curled with fear, melancholy, longing and empty.

He negotiated distance to the ground by judging the depth of blackness, and jumped. It was an awkward landing that brought soreness to his ankle. But the sprawl of Dotto's music tugged at his chest and filled it with something forlorn that was too wide to close, too steep to contain. He stood in the black night awash with the sound of her flute.

Sudden footsteps. Two voices. Dingo laughter. He pressed against the wall, held his breath.

'I need a woman,' a man's voice said.

More laughter.

'Well, this place is full of them,' a second voice. 'And there is one in there with her flute.'

'Such is her beauty, the sight of her would blind me.'

'The Mezzanine, he would castrate you before you went blind.'

'Not castrate. He would have my gizzards in a pot before pouring them out in the fields for the vultures to peck.'

'No woman comes willingly to that kind of man, no wonder he steals them.'

The footsteps were gone, taking their laughter with them.

Muntu took a breath. He burst in a sprint across the yard. The drift of music guided him towards her chamber. He dove, rolled, burst for a nearside wall and pressed against it. A westerly wind, warm and soft, brushed him on its way to the edge of the world. Two guards passed only skins from his feet, and then they were gone.

He leaned his shoulder against wood and pushed. The door gave without sound. He slipped inside. There she was, right there. Darkness shrouded half her body, her neck long and graceful as a stork's. She played music of orange sun and yellow stars, radiant

23

rays and glowing tips. The drone of her song told of wind and birds and men and green forest. Light from her lamp, one he had never seen, cast silver to her hair, added texture to each strand, softened contrast as tresses fell to bare buttocks.

His tread was soft, wishing to surprise. He touched her shoulder, and the flute's notes fell to silence.

'My heart,' he said.

She stiffened, half-turned.

He gazed, not at a teardrop face with diamond eyes, but the pale, yellow face of Reed or Dolphin, one of the chief's new wives. They eyed each other, his astonishment, her terror and then indignation. She let the flute fall, covered her nudity with a palm and screamed.

In that instant, a whistle blew. As a thunder of feet raced towards the hut, he understood. The frightened woman was neither Reed nor Dolphin, the chief's young wives. It was Loquat, the new bride stolen from Dumay two sleeps ago. As her cry invaded his senses, as its ringing caused throb to his ears, he swirled, leapt, and ran out of the hut.

Something large jumped from darkness and grabbed his waist. Muntu twirled and smashed a fist that connected. The next guard was built like a croc. Muntu fought, but the guard held fast. They grappled, rolled. Muntu kicked, leapt clear and ran into a burst of fresh footsteps. The last thing he saw before black cloud was the skull of a club made of acacia.

When guards dragged a half-conscious Muntu past her door, Dotto slept through the commotion. She was wrapped in dreams of streams and magnolias and light. Softness touched her naked thigh and she sighed and locked her palms, swathed in a sleep filled with a man who throbbed like the sea.

Before she could wash sleep from her face, before she could break her fast, before wind of her lover's fate could touch her, Chief Mezzanine sent her under escort to a cousin's hospitality in Burnt Bush country.

5.

Darkness lifted from his head. A white moon drifted in the frowning sky he could not help but face, moon that shone past the break of dawn. This was a bad omen, moon at sunlight. It was worse than a twin omen. He tugged his hands and sensed no feeling. Matter of fact, he could not find them. Nor could he find his fingers. A quiver of fear touched him, right up his spine. Needles sharp as elephant thorn pressed his soles. Slowly, awakening reached him. He dimly remembered racing across the yard before a guard jumped from the night, and then there were more guards and someone zonked him with a club to the head. He realised where he was. Bound hands and feet on the branch of a twisted coolabah tree. Hung upside down like a butcher bird's catch.

6.

A drum summoned the villagers. Slowly, crowds gathered.

Chief Mezzanine, a tiny man, came out in full paraphernalia. One hand clutched a new plumage diadem on his head that was as ill-fitting and resplendent as his robe embroidered in gold. The headdress carried rich colours of flame and teal. The chief stood on a dais, preening himself before the people of the land who observed him with frank curiosity. Whispers rose to a buzz of noise, the chief's compound was throbbing. He snatched silence with a beckon of hand. To the guards, he motioned the prisoner, no longer bound on the gnarled branch of a Coolabah, be brought. Villagers eyed the captive with interest and fear, and wondered at his crime.

The chief looked at the man standing before him, a man of granite and marble eyes who said nothing. A guard tried to retrieve the opal stone from the man's neck, but cried out in pain, the stone aglow when a stranger touched it. The guard's hand was left charred where it had touched the stone.

'What have you to say for yourself?' demanded Chief Mezzanine.

Opal eyes gave him nothing. They focused at a point in space.

'Have you no fear?' cried the chief. 'Speak when I speak to you, for I have power to save you.'

The man said nothing.

'Any more insolence and I will have you buried in sand to your neck for flesh worms to feed upon.' The chief swept his arms at the crowd: 'Let the people hear your defence!'

The prisoner said nothing.

The black opal amulet felt warm on his skin. The shard of fear that had touched Muntu when he saw crowds flock like a bird parade – fear he tried best not to show – was gone.

Now, gazing above the chief's head to a place between the flamboyant plume hat and an evil-boding moon in the sky, he saw a vision, an infinity of beauty. Dotto stood before him dressed in nothing but a face veil of silver cobweb. Through it, dazzling promise shone in her eyes. Her nipples stood sharp, straight as truth. Seeing her, he was struck with awe, with silence. The silhouette of her hands reached out to him in a slow dance, lit by ambient light that came from something surreal, light that bounced in shimmers on her blue head. Suddenly, he knew. She was dead. His Dotto was dead. With the same knowledge, he accepted mortality. He was going to meet his bride.

'I know this man,' said a voice in the crowd. 'He is a man of peace. His name is Muntu.'

'I know this name,' another said. 'He is the great grandson of Kuntu.'

'The banished medicine man who defied your great grandfather's crowning,' yelled another.

The chief nearly gagged. 'An outcast!' he cried, indignant.

A guard pacified him with a gourd of corn brew. Mildly calmed, Chief Mezzanine addressed the crowd: 'This man stands bold and defiant, but he has broken tradition.'

He looked at Muntu.

This time Muntu looked back at him.

'I ask —' Chief Mezzanine tried a different tone. 'I ask: why do you seek to defile my daughter?'

Muntu spoke. 'You should know more about defiling than I.'

'Descendant of a cockroach!'

'The only cockroach I see has eyes as shifty as the lyrebird plumage on his head.'

The crowd heckled.

Chief Mezzanine roared. 'Guard! Hit this man!'

Before a bewildered guard could lift his hand, the prisoner spoke. 'Do you not know how to do it?'

'Hit him hard!'

But long after Muntu spoke, his words rang deep as a wind horn across the crowd, though they still heckled.

So to make an example of the man with granite eyes who dared speak back, Chief Mezzanine ordered his punishment.

Flutes, harps and banjos. It was a carnival. Celebration rang from one corner to another. Children danced, wrapped in loin clothes and sisal wraps and cloaks of vibrant colours.

Marksmen stood ten lengths away. They tested their spear throwers and dipped the nose of each spear into black gum melt. They dipped the gummed spears into a pot of fire, until the tips blazed.

At the chief's signal, *sizzzhhh!*

Burning spears soared into a rack of wood and grass where fire burnt. Its belly throbbed, ever so white, its lip danced, orange as ginger. Inside the flames, tongues licked a man's skin, cooked him whole. It was a ritual execution to expunge.

A boomerang drum drowned the villagers' song. A harp soaked the cries of a yellow-tailed cockatoo mating outside the chief's walls.

Chief Mezzanine's voice lifted across the fire, pleading, almost frightened, for despite his bravado he was a coward. 'I can save you, arrogant fool. Plead for mercy and I will order the fire be put out.'

There was no sound of Muntu. No cry, no plea.

Tongues of fire licked the stack, a blaze that burnt furiously, keen as lust. A cloud of black smoke enveloped and stung nostrils. It smothered flamboyantly garbed children now clutched to their mothers.

The lucky stone calmed him. It was his protective stone; it would keep him from harm. It had once belonged to the great medicine man – his kindred named Kuntu. Fear had no place here.

Dotto was waiting for him. Soon, her face would press against his back, tender arms wrapped around him. He felt himself spreading, filling with heat. He used mental powers, the gift of his ancestors, to diminish pain. Whatever happened now, it was almost over.

His soul floated on a sea of green.

It was over.

But... then he noticed his black opal amulet, the one that had saved him from the flames... It was gone.

Then he heard a groan. Looked around but knew that the sound had come from him, from lips caught in a burning stack below. Another soul was still caught in that body. A soul that yearned to be free. The amulet had released... a twin soul?

He looked down again at the white flames. Saw what the people of the land could not see from deep smoke. The knots holding his body had burned and broken away. He looked above the tidal waves of the vast sea beyond and caught no glimpse of Dotto. As disquiet touched him, nothingness began to spread. A vast nothing swept across him. He was falling, falling.

Right into the lip of a giant void.

7.

So the people of the land did not see the condemned man's tethers fall. But what they saw, they shook their heads retelling it many years to come. A dancing man engulfed in flame leapt from the burning stack. He grunted like a beast and ran towards them, orange-mad tongues licking his hair. Villagers fell back as one, people crying out, confused.

The body ran, heedless of its burning head, heedless of its spirit.

Before people could register shock, there, in the heart and soul of festivity, where boomerang drums pounded *pom! pi! boom!*, escorting a soul to a different world, the body fell to the ground, engulfed in flames, arms and feet dancing. Fire had eaten half its face, singed its brows. Already, blisters were popping. Finally, when the body ceased thrashing and only its spirit twitched to be free, somebody cried, 'Harlequna!', above the stench of charred flesh.

So the people of the land were left to improvise. Death could be slowed. Or hastened. In a bid to free the dying man's trapped spirit, they doused him with eucalyptus oil, tossed dried twigs on him, added gum tar to feed his fire.

He glowed like a shooting star. And when there was nothing but a mound of ash sprawled in the shape of a man, flecks still smouldered with every touch of new wind.

The black opal was never found.

Later, much later, and secretly, when the day moon retired, when stars filled its space until they dimmed to twilight, two women, defiled daughters now wives of a coward, scooped what ash remained before a northerly wind could scatter it. They put it in a calabash and stole it to a sacred place where they buried what was left of Muntu.

There he lay, a single soul separated from his twin, next to the bones of his forefather, the Great Chief Goanna who saved his country from the greed of a settler who wanted a mall, a restaurant and a spa retreat in the burial grounds of the forefathers.

Chief Mezzanine lowered his lyrebird eyes and staggered back. He turned his face and threw up on his toes. He had only wanted to scare the fool, but arrogance had made things happen. A courier from the Burnt Bush country where Dotto was exiled found him face in his hands, pissed as a newt.

'Your daughter,' the messenger said. 'She drank root poison.'

8.

And so, following the burning of an innocent man, a man whose crime was simply the love of a twin, a man himself of twin souls generated by a lucky stone, the bones of Great Chief Goanna stirred in their grave.

News of the grisly death, of a man cooked to the hilt, sent shockwaves among tribes near and far. Before his tribe could travel north and avenge Muntu, the Valley of Dreams took its own revenge. Enraged at the people of the land who had done a terrible deed, it froze its roots. Stems of purple magnolias and bright red poinsettias that encouraged the place of dreams choked. The thin leaves of ball spinifex, the tubular flowers of velvet kangaroo paw, the dancing leaves of the olive holly – they all shrivelled. Before long, land became parched. Despite two rain seasons, it grew full of boulders and dust that blinded.

Barren soil replaced grass once so soft, so green, that in better days villagers had slept outdoors on its felt beds. Thorns replaced evergreen leaves. Buds fell away from mother plants, which in turn groaned and collapsed. The sun bared itself and reflected its face so harshly that the smaller creatures of the land died or fled. Forked trees stood with bark so raspy, children could not climb.

Anthills choked with heat and dust, only nests of bees remained. So the Valley of Dreams, destined for something finer, sought a cleaner world, one whose sun did not char its surface but made happy rainbows on the ground.

The first volcano took a thousand deaths. Then stressed and distressed soil shook itself off the ground and rifted. The holes it left swallowed scores more, man and beast. The moon changed and grew sharper, rounder, bigger, whiter – as though distance had varied between Earth and Sun.

Dingo cries filled the air. Mobs of kangaroos and wallabies hopped away, away… Snakes slithered from whatever bush was left and invaded homesteads where they did not bite; they just appeared dazed, frightened. Even galahs no longer swarmed to attack the grubs on sun mats.

The world was changing.

The end of the world as people knew it came with no warning. The two women who had buried the burning stumps in the Valley of Dreams were as astonished as the rest of them in Northern Country when more land, not content at swallowing scores, grew moodier. Violent movement of the Earth's surface broke its crust deep and wide. Cracks and fissures appeared, trapping villagers in crevices between walls, and the deaths now appeared to be targeting Chief Mezzanine's circle. The chief and his unfortunate guards and harem sank into a fissure.

Suddenly, suddenly! The land tore itself from roots and rock. It rose above hills and valleys. It took with it the two women who had buried what was left of Muntu, and a few villagers who had not partaken in the ritual, including one Mama Pebble. The land elevated itself, soared in a straight line of infinite movement, beyond two asteroid belts, to a space within the moon's orbit in ancient terrain that joined a galaxy of independents.

Here, it tucked itself – with its hidden treasure, a black opal that kept its bearer from harm – and made a new habitat.

9.

Stars in the new habitat changed shape. They became triangular. Then they changed to petals, then diamonds, then oval, then rings and back to stars. Soon they became obsolete.

Sound became tri-colour and flooded, rainbow as a Lorikeet.

Night was no longer determined by darkness, moonlight and a glimmer of stars. Lunar months were things of the past. There were few inhabitants in that terrain where rhythm of day and night slowed, where sun, moon or stars never faded day or night, and all they knew was that their world held many colours of the spectrum. There were no more pale flowers; it was a remarkable world.

They evolved into a new species of ivory eyes and purple hair to withstand the climate. There, without chief or culture or tradition, they lived isolated lives. They tried to grow anemones and azaleas and alstroemerias and red berry and holly and freesias and Dutch tulips... Anything to remind them of Earth. But the soil was red as the sun, stubborn too; it bred only grubs that bled milk. Sweet lizards that tasted like peanut-coated meat. So instead of creating a new Earth, the new inhabitants sang of Earth, songs that fed the new galaxy so that it blossomed.

They sang of the white sun and golden stars, of shimmering tips and a green sea that throbbed. They sang of gods who visited people and listened to their laments. Their songs grew lavish.

They sang of Great Chief Goanna who parted molecules from the waters of the sea. Molecules that spread to the sea's bed between tidelines and swept the settlers off their feet until they drowned.

They sang of Kuntu, the medicine man who defied the great grandfather of Chief Mezzanine – who had the eyes of a lyrebird. Chief Mezzanine who grew under the thumb of his mother, a woman with no maternal bone in her body, with a poison chalice for a tongue and she created a brute with capacity for theft and murder.

They sang of dazzling Dotto, whose skin was soft as a river bed, whose eyes shone like a diamond.

They sang of Muntu become a god, the tallest, most beautiful man, who gleamed with animal fat and from whose body sunbeams danced. He was a creature of light who absorbed energy from the sun, and he looked with calm arrogance at coward Chief Mezzanine and said, 'Do you not know how to do it?'

They sang of wilderness birds and oasis forest, of hilly country and cool wind islands whose scent lingered like bush mint. They sang of westerly wind, warm and soft. Of northerly wind, fiercer than its cousin. Of grubs and sweet lizards.

And because the gods were kind, because they listened, they granted the people their wishes. Rains fell, and life began anew. With life came bandicoots, bilbies, wombats, echidnas, platypus, koalas, emus, wallabies, roos and crocs. Anemones, azaleas, alstroemerias, holly, freesias, red berry, tulips and magnolias.

10.

One day an elder of the native people of the land was bushwalking when something stubbed his toe, and he cried out. An amulet. It glowed like bright orange fire and the ground around it pulsed with a heartbeat.

He had walked this path a thousand times and nothing had stubbed his toes. Today, this special stone had pushed itself from the Earth's heart for him, just him, to find.

He picked it up and the stone felt warm to touch. It changed colour from orange to red to black when he looked at it from different angles. As he continued to look, the flame in its heart ebbed. And then it was just a stone: a black opal that allowed him to claim it. He noticed that his bleeding toe had come whole, as if never injured.

The amulet became an heirloom – cherished for its healing, its fire and intuition – handed down through generations by the elders of the people.

Four: The Beast in a Calabash

1.

In the world of a new species of ivory eyes and purple hair, right there in the Valley of Dreams, lived Mama Pebble.

Her tongue was sharp as a thorn, faster than a boomerang: 'Belly like pregnant ants yous fish face slobs its time yous be responsible childrens not act like grubs with crushed heads! Make no play or I make example of yous and yous fly like possums with no tails!'

And when she wasn't yowling, temper and tongue gone wild, she had answers for everything.

'Why they call yous Pebble?' a man would ask.

It was dawn, she said. Having tormented her pregnant mother three days, three nights, a breakfast and half a lunch, the child resisted the midwives' attempts to prod her out.

'Midwife she pull and poke and beg and curse, and mamma she claw and crow and clench and yowler. Midwife she finally squeeze me from belly with three wooden ladles and I pop. Mamma she take one look at me and faint. Papa he take one

35

look, two look and he hold me upside down as I yowled. Me face
go cherry and he say, 'Baby is one ugly something, face tight as
fist look like stone, she be call Pebble.'

'But if yous was one ugly,' the man said, 'where it all go? That
ugly?'

'Gods be good. Me make them no angry so me skin age slow
remain soft as wallaby oil and me face tight as seal.'

'And why yous twin boys name cheeta boys?'

'Because boys be destine be something this world never
forget.'

And though she guessed the truth of her words, and of her
powers, how could she sense things that were yet to happen?

Years ago, when she started seeing things, they were all dead
people. Once it was the Great Chief Goanna himself. There he
was, resplendent in kangaroo skin and emu feathers, opals and
damn-all. He stood without word by her bedside and shadows
circled his eyes. When in half a daze she lifted her palm to touch
him, he thinned and vanished.

Sometimes, she saw animals. All dead as wood yet alive.
Creatures from a place of dreams: grubs seeping cooking juice.
Crocs dripping wetting blood and what else. One thing they had
in common, they were creatures she had gobbled only nights
before. In her seeing, the animals were not minding their own
selves and running about the yard, or scaring her own self and
forcing her to scurry, they simply stood and stared solemnly by
her bedside. And when they spoke, they asked why she had eaten
them.

She pelted them with twigs, ladles, stones…

They ducked and returned with one question: why, why had
she eaten them? When there were too many of them speaking all
at once in animal and spirit speak and she could no longer split
one word from another, sound became a blur, and she swooned.

So she became a strict vegetarian and ate yams, mandisa pine
nuts, weeds, roots, shoots, cabbage palm leaves, and pretty much
anything green, purple, orange or yellow with attachment to the

soil. But she still fed her twins meat: grub, lizard, galah, bandicoot, bilby, chicken, numbat, possum, croc... perhaps that was why her visions never stopped. She had long overcome the disappointment of not having girls and was content the cheeta boy twins were there to distract her from the persistence of nocturnal dead animals.

And though the twins found themselves in a pickle every now and then, they were her boys, seemingly shallow but in truth intelligent, judging from their ability to get away from trouble despite their shenanigans. When the boys were of good manners, she rubbed emu fat into their hair until it dazzled. She told them about souls that wept blood, dead things come to visit.

She told them about dead Chief Goanna who came one night and stood all resplendent by her bedside. She told them about all the meat creatures that made a blur of sound until she swooned. She told them about the place of dreams: 'Sacred land where them bones of spirit lie next to Great Chief Goanna of old.' It was a forbidden land that the boys well knew never to visit.

2.

It was the height of noon one day between dry and wet season. The twins were approaching their twelfth cycle, trapped between the cusp of boyhood and manhood. They painted war on their faces and tormented the little girl next door – they nearly pulled the amethyst from her braids and only paused when she cried. They snuck into the neighbour's yard and sneaked grubs from his pot, but he found them in the act and he cursed them. They ran laughing and streaked what remained of the war paint on Mama Pebble's cleanly swept floor and raced out, still laughing, to the yard where they crushed honey ants with their thumbs until their mother chased them with a whip. They knew it was wrong to hurt people or creatures of the gods, but mischief had filled in for boredom.

One thing that always distracted them from silliness was food. They liked eating, and gobbled just about anything, but they had fed and their stomachs were tightly ballooned above their loin cloths. Because they were bored and life was much better without rules, they raced like beasts, yelped in half-formed voices caught between childhood and adolescence, raced and giggled.

They were still full of play when they yanked the tails of Mama Pebble's corn rows. She slapped their cheeky hands from her head but that deterred them only for a moment. So she dragged them by the ear to her war-painted hut. And though they struggled and her back had lost its straightness, though her hands were wet with emu oil and still smelt of the chook's neck she had wrung only moments before, her wrists held firm.

There, on painted ground, she sat the boys down and rebuked them. 'Yous cheeta boys of age now but still running about tomfoolering. Make one more mischief and I make example of yous as they did that poor man that done Chief Mezzanine's daughter, they do him true.'

'Tell us the story' the twins cried, although they had heard it umpteen times before.

So she told them the story, told it in startling detail as always, starting with land that had been. Land that tore itself from Earth when a terrible deed was done. Land that lifted itself and lived amongst a rainbow of independent galaxies. Land inhabited by a new people that neighboured the spartan *Visio* who were unbeatable in battle, the back-footed *Que* who ran faster than the wind, and the three-eyed *Anchors* who had such profound gifts of the 'seeing', a gift that the new purple-haired inhabitants soon learnt but quickly lost, save for a handful.

She was just getting into the tale when their minds began to wander.

'I hungry, Ma,' Ku said.

'But yous just eaten, stole from the neighbour his grub.'

'Grub thin like spinifex leaf,' said Doh.

'Taste like coolabah bark,' said Ku.

'I hungry,' they cried in unison.

But Mama Pebble snapped her fingers and said, 'Listen, yous!'

And they did. Listen. They sat like kidney beans, bellies cloaked with orange dirt, and received her tale as usual, only today with less sombreness. Matter of fact, they laughed, and that was indulgence, for they could do worse.

'Yous understand this story?' Mama Pebble asked.

'Ahm,' the twins said with twinkling eyes.

'It funny story?'

'Ahm.' The laughter was full of hiccups.

'Mama Pebble sure tell some story,' one twin said.

'She tell it to make fear,' another said.

'Yous think it make true?'

'Not all.' And they laughed.

Mama Pebble slipped off a leather thong and flew it at them.

They ducked in a twink and showed her their tongues.

'Foolhardy children I make example of yous until yous gobble like turkey!'

'Ahm.'

Foolhardy children dodged her hands and, heads full of empty, fled out of the gateless posts that stood useless like discharged sentries, down a dirt road, where they tumbled across a parched field, raced through another meadow and out into wilderness.

3.

Ku pounded behind Doh, who was faster by a pace. They ran themselves ragged, cutting through golden grass of familiar land until they were in unfamiliar territory, all the way from home in the sacred grounds at the edge of the valley.

Ku leaned forward, hands on his knees, and tried to get some breath back. 'Messing about sacred place bring bad luck.'

Doh turned his head and laughed. 'Yous pigeon.'

'Yous pigeon,' Ku said. 'Mama Pebble she catch us, we trouble.'

'Pigeon.'

'Don't game me.'

'Scared-pigeon-scared-pigeon-scared-pigeon.'

'Yous a duck head.' Ku gave his twin a tap on the head.

'Scared-pigeon-scared-pigeon-scared-pigeon.'

Ku fought him to the ground. They fell, a tangle of hands and feet.

Doh finally cried from under Ku, who rolled off. Doh peeled from the ground, spitting dust and twigs. Something hard underfoot stilled him. 'Look what I find.'

'What?'

'Calabash.' Doh crouched low and peered.

'Maybe not calabash.'

'I say calabash.'

'Let me.' Ku pushed past Doh.

'No. Me.' Doh pushed back. He kicked the protruding rib, tugged, it gave. It was... yes, a calabash. He raised it in his hands. 'It warm.' He flung it. 'It hot.' He stared at the residue in his hands.

The boys stood very quiet.

'What his name again? Man that done Chief Mezzanine's girl?'

'He name Muntu. Why?'

Doh pointed at horizontal markings carved with a stone knife on the neck of the thing.

'It say Mu –'

VOOPFH... the calabash jumped from the ground. *Voopfh!* The calabash bounced up swift as anger with a sound so ominous, the boys fell. The object soared above their heads. *Voopfh!* As the calabash came crashing down, the boys screamed.

There, on sacred ground, a monstrous wing of black lifted from the neck of the calabash. It stood large as a twisted coolabah tree, branches swaying to a rampant northerly wind. It smelt like charred grub and rotten cabbage palm leaves. It formed and deformed like bees or smoke. Suddenly it roared. The sound was horrific, and it finished in thunder.

The tree morphed into the smoky shape of a man who mushroomed several feet above ground and dribbled soot. Slowly, the shape lifted and soared towards the sky, its form breaking and joining in little ash clouds until it vanished.

Flecks of black and a blended odour of spit fire, rubbish pit and burnt flesh covered the boys.

The soil was still hot a few paces surrounding the area. But the ground had sealed itself from where the calabash lifted.

The twins glanced at each other.

Doh was the first to find his voice. 'Did? Yous? See?'

4.

Mama Pebble stirred a pot of bubbling broth with a wooden ladle. As she swirled the liquid, she saw her sons racing home from the distance.

Doh galloped steady and fast. Ku pounded a pace behind.

A red sky chased them all the way home.

Mama Pebble lifted an ancient face and stared at the furious whirl, and wondered. The red sky was now a hurricane or a bushfire that up close turned out to be a billow of dust. It tumbled and spun after the twins. It halted just short of the boys, the yard, the three-stone hearth and the bubbling pot.

The boy twins stamped into the yard. To Mama Pebble's bewilderment, Doh burst into tears. Crying was a thing he had not done since constipation bothered his walk, and Mama Pebble wrestled him to the ground, ripped his loin cloth and scooped out a rocky turd with her middle finger, and the boy roared fit to kill. But Mama Pebble parted his buttock cheeks and rubbed possum oil inside. Now the boy cried worse than he did then.

Ku half-sat on his knees and he too burst into tears. Crying was something he had not done since Mama Pebble jumped on him in elephant grass during a call of nature, a sharpened stone knife in her fist, and bulled him to the ground, spread his legs with her knees, and nipped the foreskin off his wazoo. As he squirmed and bit his tongue, which added insult to wound, he wailed in the language of his forefathers that it hurt worse than the prick of a poisoned thorn. But Mama Pebble rubbed grub salve into the searing, bound it with banana bark.

Now with their crying, she searched their heels for the bite of a taipan or a copperhead or a scorpion, but found nothing. So she did not dash for a snake stone to draw out any poison and, instead, knelt by the twins.

'Tell Mama Pebble what be wrong why yous cry what be wrong —' Her words froze with her touch of Doh's arm.

There was a roar, as if from the horizon, and it echoed twice. The world dimmed, if only for a moment, and it looked like someone had turned off the daylight. As light flooded back, just then, Mama Pebble keeled towards the ground, foaming at the lips.

The twins abandoned their crying and Ku spoke first.

'She touch beast dust on yous from calabash.'

They stood in unbearable silence watching her seizure. When she stopped convulsing, white beads dribbled down her cheek in unparallel formations. Her eyes opened wide. The boys sought an oasis in them, one they had known all their lives, and found none. Through a glistening of tears, she looked at the cheeta boy twins with blurred eyes.

She smiled and said the last thing she heard from the boys: 'Ahm.'

The twins looked at each other.

'She gone mad.'

'Messing about sacred place bring bad luck. We sick now.'

5.

Inside the valley of dreams, one day the sky roared and broke its silence anew. Sound became tri-colour, lemon, plum and sapphire;

the moon changed its shape and became a sphere. Folk with ankle-length amethyst hair watched this full moon that dazzled until a mushroom wisp blackened the horizon. A strange smoke dimmed the lunar glow, ahead of a chase of clouds red as port.

Together, the clouds and the mushroom swept above an olive field, a dirt road, and a golden meadow. Mama Pebble, the ancient woman struck by a curse, turned half-blind eyes to the phenomenon in the sky. She nodded unfazed and turned her attention to a woven rug bearing twirls of sun-dried grub.

The twin boys paused from twiddling and meddling, parrying with shields, and watched the mushroom cloud in petrified silence. They remembered the beast that soared from the rib of a calabash, an ash man who sprinkled charcoal that brought madness to Mama Pebble.

But now, instead of soaring and bellowing above them as it had done before, the thing from the skies tumbled towards wilderness.

'Did? Yous? See?'

The boys leapt and chased the cloud. They ran to the end of the world and watched the swirl half a world away. There, in the distance, it swept inside the moon's orbit and crossed to neighbouring *Que*, the land of the back-footed people.

6.

Parched from its protracted trek, the spirit formed and deformed, never here, never there. It sprinkled above trees and forests, and finally swooped into a village. Inside a cluster of cottages with crumbling walls, a couple strained against each other. The woman saw it first. The man looked over his shoulder too late, as something ripped into him.

The surge of killings carried through the tribes of the spartan *Visio*, and then the three-eyed *Anchors*. Finally, bewildered at not finding its twin, the mystical creature abandoned the galaxies and descended to Earth.

7.

That is how it was.

The cheeta-boy-twins live to this day, trapped in childhood, in keeping with the ethos of the tale. They continue parrying with sticks, scheming and twirling with agility and athletics. Twice or thrice a score, when the moon rises full and dazzling, when ever so slowly it begins to dim and disappears, and it casts a shadow upon the earth, the twins run to the edge of their world, looking for a glimpse of a cursed spirit, a misplaced spirit, same spirit that brought madness to Mama Pebble when she caught flecks of it on Doh's arm.

Though the end remains uncertain, memory of the beginning is not lost. Now, as one spirit floats in nothingness, yenning for his Dotto, another sweeps the galaxies, roaming from southerly shores to easterly tips, a confused demon freed from the rib of a calabash.

It seeks a twin. And water to quench its fire.

Five: The Detective

1.

And so, there was a beast. Right here on Earth.

It perched on the topmost steeple of an arched gateway into Sin Palace. It was a red-eyed demon in a crouch. Its body disintegrated and came together like a swarm of bees, ashy specks that hovered in the horizon, forming and deforming in overlapping shapes, casting shadows above the guest house that was once a church building.

Two men swung hand in hand that balmy night. They shared a laugh, and its loudness silenced the night. They paused for a dusk-induced, booze-fuelled moment of passion before crossing the arched gateway into the Gothic building. Access was by a clandestine doorbell just below a psychedelic stained-glass window of St Bridget and her plump leg crushing the head of a serpent. Double solid doors each carved with a cross into the wood swung open, swung shut. It was a priceless entry by membership only, an entry into privacy that was a promise.

Straight spliffs, hard shots in a room that was once a vestry. As the lights dimmed and the men strained against each other, they failed to notice the odour of smoke and rot that entered the room and the shapeshifting silhouette that hovered above them and sprinkled cinders upon them.

2.

And then there was Operation Limelight.

So after the man who was tall as a mandisa pine, graceful as a kudu, a beautiful man dark as night who lived in the land of Great Chief Goanna, there was a story that had a beast come to Earth.

The epilogue starts here, right now.

It opens with a flight: one that filled Detective Inspector Ivory Tembo with ashes and lead. She felt colourless and washed-out, a lead boulder in her stomach. She had no faith in the journey's purpose but had exhausted all options. A murderer was out there, slaying men and scattering peanuts in women's heads – they were disoriented, every single one of them; couldn't get a word out of anyone – and Operation Limelight was light-years from cracking the case.

In Ivory's mind, death was a splash of colour: claret speckled with cinders. This is what she saw in every scene associated with the killings: sprays of rich red, traces of ash.

It tickled Bahati, indulged him even, that she would explore his theory based on a myth.

'It's simple,' he said. 'Track down the seer.'

'In Orange Desert?' she said.

'In Orange Country.'

'And why should I believe you?'

'My professorship? That sagely knowhood of native studies?' he said half jokily, half grave.

Seer, medium, medicine woman – what did it matter?

But it did. Matter. Witchcraft never solved crime.

3.

As the plane droned on rough ground, ready for take-off, she remembered the story Bahati told her from his childhood, the one of the plant-hunting ceremony in the wilderness country, the calling out to the mandisa pine to give up her cones.

The plane rocked on the runway, slogged its speed, and turned. It juddered to a halt. One minute passed. Two. Seven. After an interminable wait, the plane dipped her nose and began moving again.

Ivory leaned her elbows on the armrests, glad for three seats to herself. Before long, the sink in her belly, the knot in her gut, the dullness in her ears from slant and altitude, it all vanished. She gazed at an aerial view of Sydney: trees like shrubs. Lego houses that became matchstick houses. A cobalt water map swayed with snowy surf along a golden coastline. The metropolis reduced to specks, shards of blue, grey, silver... Then it was gone, swallowed in fog. Strips of cloud drew near, nearer... The plane slipped in and out of them like a lover. Down below, a hoary carpet furrowed in cushy bumps.

Ivory ran fingers through ink black hair that gleamed with lustre. She toyed with the black amulet she wore around her neck. Today, unusually, it warmed to her touch, soothed.

Sudden fatigue from months of investigation dissipated. Calm washed through her. Deep emerald eyes grew small, smaller... Eyes that were a sharp contrast to her burnt honey skin. She was always an anomaly – her last thoughts as she succumbed to a valley of dreams splattered with crimson gore, lined with de-skinned corpses.

A stroke of sun awakened her. She opened her eyes to layers of orange and white, chameleon sun on the horizon vacillating between hues, dimming to white between bunches of cloud; popcorn cloud scrunched into fists; clouds shafting through a sea of blue; clouds like golden islands, thousands of them. They gave way to a blood-red horizon where the sun shone fiercely on a barren stretch of orange land miles, miles out.

4.

A girl from the native people of Orange Country, she was perhaps nineteen or twenty years of age, with a forest of auburn hair whose colour was mostly a coating of dirt, met her as arranged.

'Pepper Coona,' said the wilderness child with dopey eyes. 'That my name.' She eyed the amulet Ivory wore but said nothing.

Ivory forced her gaze on the girl's face, avoiding half-formed breasts hung bare. She smiled, stretched her arm. 'Ivory Tembo.'

The girl's clasp was concrete. 'Tembo.'

Ivory laughed. She had never questioned her darker skin, but other people did, in the foster homes they did, and it wasn't kind. But she understood the girl was not referring to the shade of her skin. 'It's my everything name. You're a desert child?'

'We go.'

'Pepper.' Their eyes met. 'I am grateful.' Apricot eyes, cracked lips chalk white… her simplicity was childlike. 'You came all this way to meet me.'

The girl shrugged.

A wave of uncertainty touched Ivory. Perhaps it was not after all a good idea to use a tracer she knew nothing of. Bahati's source, a native elder named Pygo who also taught at the university, was naturally reticent. As for Ivory's boss, Grant Pugley, he would not be amused by the unauthorised gallivant. She could just about see the superintendent's bulldog face all scrunched up, his mouth downward curled, hear his bark all incessant, each word a cantankerous 'arf-arf' to impatient ears.

But Ivory's visit was also a curiosity. Her mother, on her deathbed, had scribbled a name.

5.

For all her simplicity, the girl powered the car, a battered ute cloaked with layers of dust all carroty, across rugged terrain. Such was her ability to manoeuvre the vehicle across raw cuts on weather-whipped land that Ivory's admiration inched a notch high, doubled, tripled.

Anyhow, she mused, Pepper was a girl from Orange Country; she knew the terrain well. *Non sequitur,* she corrected herself. Being a good tracer did not make one a good driver. And the girl's steep silence unnerved.

'Have you met Ginny Mo'unga?' Ivory said, to initiate conversation.

'Nghh?'

'Ginny.' Ivory leaned forward. She smiled her encouragement. 'The medicine woman.'

'You look inside medicine woman eye, you die.'

Ivory drew back. She took a moment and collected herself. 'How long is the drive to Orange Crater?'

'Bottlefly like beast.'

Ivory slumped into her seat. 'Impossible,' under her breath.

'Nghh?'

So Ivory gazed out the window. Without air-conditioning, sweat was tepid, soaky. It clung. The conditions were unbearable.

The ute juddered through blank vastness, a sea of loneliness inside edges of rock. It drove alongside a wilderness of moving swamp, past a procession of fiery trees, their leaves flaming red. It swept past more foliage that bore a maudlin look – hanging branches like brooding lips. The ute turned into crimson desert dappled with blue oases – mirages; sped towards a blood-red scorcher on the horizon.

6.

Heat steeped. It sizzled in airy waves. Every now and then a burst of melancholy cries from sun baked galahs overhead invaded the harsh stillness in monotonous landscape punctuated with bull dust.

Pepper Coona parked without notice in the middle of god-forsaken bleakness and took a pit stop in clumps of spinifex. Back in the ute she manoeuvred the wheel with unwashed hands across an equally dirty countryside.

They came to a winding road.

Pepper steered resolutely round a steep curve. She nearly lost (and regained) the wheel three times, and they just about dangled on a precipice. Ivory was ready to climb out of the grunting carrot car and up the goddamn hill herself when the road began a slow wind down.

Finally – finally! – they slid into a sultry night at the end of a dust road inside a desolate crater in a place named *Maddening*. Here, the moon was big and bright. A spatter of violets, white gum and yellow grass graced parts of the land. The rest of the place stood stark as a skeleton. The ute parked several feet from a wall of ghost gums surrounding a red mud house. Other than a sway of leaves in creepy foliage, the compound held no sign of life.

'Medicine woman, she live there.' Pepper Coona pointed.

'Take me.'

'Nghh?' Pepper shot a glance in the direction of grass thatch above the sombre house, rolled up the driver window and kept the car humming.

'You can do it,' Ivory tried again.

Pepper shuddered and drew arms around herself.

'But what if the medicine woman doesn't speak English?' demanded Ivory.

Pepper shook her deep auburn head, shook it again more doggedly to confirm her refusal to dislodge from the ute, and pouted into the night.

'Well! But you *are* going to wait?'

'Go!' The conclusive whisper pushed toward Ivory like a lip.

Ivory stepped away from lip, but no footpath led to the residence.

She weaved through Mitchell grass, kicked thin leaves of spinifex that speared through the dream catcher pattern in her sandals. A rustle swept across the ground. A glow of eyes shimmered from a clump. Incensed at the cracked-lip boofhead in the droning ute, Ivory trod pigeon-toed against the backward slant of hostile grass that grazed. A ball of fur leapt and hared down a hole, and that was all it took to snap Ivory's resolve. She ran and fell straight into prickly leaves clumped at the edge of a low hung mandisa pine.

She pushed the leaves and noticed her own trembling hand. Inside the canopy, two wide rows of red Kangaroo Paw led to a timber doorway.

7.

Ivory raised a scraped hand, but the door inched open before she could touch it.

'I have been waiting for you,' a voice older than Jacob said from within the pitch black.

Ivory took a step into a room plunged with darkness that stalked like a malevolent spirit. A tang of herb, a murky odour of river (and hell worse) snatched air from her nostrils, brought tightness to her chest.

'Don't gawk by the door,' Jacob Voice said. 'Enter.'

Ivory swallowed. 'I can't see you.'

'Listen to the darkness.'

Ivory's eyes acclimatised. Two rough-sawn benches stood along a rough wall next to a line of pots, the shape of a robed woman bent over them.

Ivory took one forward step and bumped her forehead against another pot on a knotted rope that fell from the roof. She flinched from a velvet brush sprawling from the swing pot.

'A platypus waddles straighter. Can you walk, or you will harm my cousin?'

'I wouldn't suppose you're referring to the potted plant as your cousin.'

'One word, and I will turn you into a bottlebrush.'

'I cannot see a goddamn thing. In the car, there's a flashlight...'

'Your forefathers carried owls in their eyes.'

A burning wick inside a lamp on the ground smoked and steadied to dim light that lifted the darkness to a strange glow. Grim air draped the room. Dark smudges on unfinished walls toyed with Ivory's imagination.

The Jacob-voiced female was young, and she wore charcoal eyes that glowed. Her study of Ivory's approach was wry. 'Sit.' A crooked finger pointed to a bench.

'I would rather stand. Are you Ginny Mo'unga?'

Natural cherry lips curled once more at the corners. 'I knew you would find us.' She eyed the amulet. 'So that's what happened to it.'

'Happened to what?'

'The amulet that was gifted or stolen.'

'It's a gift from my mother!'

'I'm sure it is. Did she tell you where it came from?' The coal in her eyes glowed.

'My mother is dead. I don't give two cents about the silly amulet.'

'Is it that silly?'

'Then take it!'

'I couldn't, if I tried. It chooses where it goes.' She eyed Ivory. 'Ever had the flu?'

'Not that I remember.'

Ginny laughed. 'Your roots. Inspector – is it?'

'Yes.'

'You will not find a crime story here, Inspector.'

'What story will I find?'

An origins story. The medicine woman's words burned in her head, even though Ginny hadn't spoken. *What did the sisters tell you?*

'How do you –?'

Sister Immaculata – she was the kindest.

8.

Ivory's legs gave. She fell on the bench. 'If you're looking for a confession –'

Your mother was some random, I'm sorry about that.

'A white teen runaway, Sister Immaculata said. She was a drug junkie.'

Spent some time with the people of the land someplace in the wilderness country. Died in childbirth, but not before she scribbled a name: Orange Crater. When the bub they pulled came out coloured, Sister Immaculata said the name was as good as a postcode. It was the amulet that surprised them all. It glowed, unfastened itself from the death mother's neck and, like a magnet, wrapped itself around the child's neck. There, it promptly unglowed. When a nurse in the juvenile detention hospital tried to touch it, the amulet charred her fingers. It quickly became clear that the amulet was no ordinary thing and was resistant to most people's touch – there was no apparent logic in its choices.

That is how Ivory got the amulet: it chose her.

Now she wondered about her mother – did she fall in love with an elder who then gave her the amulet? But why would he? Perhaps she stole it, and the amulet let her. But why would it? Perhaps it chose her mother, or Ivory, over the elder – did it know her mother was pregnant? Whatever the case, surely the amulet wouldn't let her addict mother pawn it for money. But somehow, she got some bucks. And it rekindled her penchant for drugs, which landed her in a juvie.

Ivory still struggled to think of her mother as a junkie. When she was little, she imagined her absent mother as a bird woman who travelled the worlds to find time and to contemplate the myths of a brand new body whistled in song, plucked on a ukulele that vibrated with the wind. Blunders in the notes did not disable the music and its nettles of sound shook the Earth and lifted the sea, before the bird woman swooped and hooked Ivory with her talons.

'And my father?'

Died of a broken heart.

'For losing me, the amulet or my mother?'

The seer's eyes simply burnt.

Ivory shrugged. 'I'd no idea what to expect of a medicine woman. But you've exceeded it.'

You seek my help and yet do not know what to expect?

'I am ignor –'

Is that your talisman? The woman's woollen head yellow as corn shook. *Ignorance. I sense something special in you.*

Ginny sat beside Ivory on the bottom-numbing bench. She rested her crooked finger on Ivory's hand. 'The gods! It really is you.'

'I don't get it.'

'Your father was a good man, a descendant of the Great Chief Goanna.'

Ivory stood. Her rage at the bringing up of a father she never knew shook her body. 'Whatever witchery –'

Ginny snatched upright in a blink. 'Do I cast bones?' Her coal eyes glowed. Just as suddenly, the seer's anger ebbed. She smiled sadly. 'That's the problem, right there.' Her Jacob voice grew older, tragic even. Her ageless skin carried the young scent of bush mist. 'You are expecting me to cast my bones.'

'Do the people of Orange Crater cast bones?'

'You come swinging bones expecting witchery. You're in the wrong world. I am not a night runner. And your disbelief is powerful. It overwhelms.' It was a whisper, dry at the edges.

'Teach me belief.'

'What you need more than anything is to know who you are.'

'And you will tell me?'

'To follow the path...' Ginny shook her head. 'Telling you this now is of no consequence.'

'Tell me what?'

9.

The seer was silent. And then: 'He has invaded your world.'

'Are you seeing this now?'

'Now, yesterday – why place a schedule on what I see?'

'So the evil you see is a man?'

'I could call him IT, and I did not say it is an evil.'

'You make this very difficult.'

Ginny smiled, and then grew serious. 'The men it has killed – tell me about them.'

'Spleen, innards spilled. All of them bathed in rivers of blood. It's the ash I don't understand. Sometimes there is no death for months. And then...' The crime scenes were something else. No knives, no sharp objects, no ballistic fragments, no sign of battering with a blunt object. Just victims clawed all over. Inside and out. 'And the ash when you touch it... Hard as diamonds.'

'Not everything is what it seems.'

'No screams. Nothing. Not a single witness.'

'The world is bigger than Sydney. Follow the moon's cycle.'

'Like the blood moon and the malevolence it brings?'

'You believe that shit?'

Blood moon superstition was a bit stretched, Ivory had to agree. And a lunar eclipse happens ever so rarely, and none had happened on the dawns of the murders. 'Right now, I'm ready to believe anything.'

Ginny's chest rose and fell slowly. 'These men that were butchered. Were they born… twins?'

'Yes. But how –?'

'So it does kill them,' the medicine woman said. She steepled her fingers and rested her chin on them.

'Do you know why?'

'A lost soul will get desperate.'

'I don't understand.'

'I don't expect you to. What I am saying is that it seeks a twin. Trapped in a dimension beyond the place of dreams.'

Ivory stayed silent.

'It does not mean to kill,' said Ginny. 'It feeds. The men it preys on produce something that brings hunger. It invades them to satiate itself. But, once inside, it does not know how to safely leave.'

'Pointless deaths, then,' Ivory said. 'And the women?'

'Useless to the impatient mind.'

'I can't get any sense out of them.'

'Perhaps what you need is not getting, but giving.'

'How?'

'How?'

Ivory sighed. 'Sin Palace. One of the men was a twin – he was killed. There was a survivor; he lost his mind like the women. Why?'

'Why, indeed?'

Ivory buried her head in her hands. 'Must we loop like this?'

'You ask foolish questions, daughter of the land.'

Ivory looked up. 'Then give me some answers. Can you help us?'

The medicine woman's eyes swept Ivory's knee-length pants with disdain. 'The education they gave you, does it make you white?'

Ivory lowered her eyes. 'I'm sorry. Teach me to ask the right questions.'

'I knew of your visit before anyone told me of it. My door opened before you knocked. And yet you ask if I can help?'

10.

Unclued to history, having been abandoned by a girl with apricot eyes, Detective Inspector Ivory Tembo was forced to spend the night in the shack of an ageless medicine woman.

She wore fatigue to her bed and lay curved like an ancient blade, listening to voices of blood memory, delinquents and insomniacs with no false security of body, just self-inflicted mutilations infected with self-doubt. And, like the inner child she was, she listened and listened for a mother's voice but heard nothing, just the ragged breath of sleep far out in an orange desert. There was a secret nail in her core, and it crucified her over and over with reminders of her orphanage, the testimony of her solitude. Her marrow did not remember where her ancestry rose, feeling its way to her otherness. It did not remember the colour of a mother's eyes, the silk and sandpaper of a father's stubble or the wet kiss of a breast's milk. All it remembered was the tear, the yank of an umbilical cord from a womb, and then falling, falling into careless space and knitted together by strangers.

She dreamt of Bahati and his naturally drowsy eyes that reminded her of a koala's. In his hands he held a glass of soda and rum.

'The little green shoots from the mandisa pine make the best smoke,' he said without speaking. Words seeped in colours – orange and limes – from his mind to her head like osmosis.

She woke up to the face of a strange woman standing by her bedside.

'Let us go to Sydney,' Jacob Voice said, tight as a drum skin. 'The buntu has killed again.'

Six: Operation Limelight

1.

She woke up in scrub country, not to dear Bahati and his curls but to the face of an ageless seer by her bed. Ginny dug sweet bananas from a hole in the corner of the hut, and they made tracks under a sky silvered with dawn. Ginny walked with a digging stick, a gourd and two pouches on her neck, half a limp and a tread that Ivory worked hard to keep up with.

They walked miles, miles out in blistering heat until more than a niggle claimed Ivory's ankle. She massaged the pressure points in her soles to relieve them, but her walk refused to settle into a steady rhythm, particularly with the sandals she wore.

No wonder she went silent. Ahead, cruising in leather thongs, the impossible medicine woman seemed to step it up despite her limp, and left behind a trail of dust that dirtied Ivory. Swatting bottle flies this way and that, Ivory was grateful when a gentle wind blew, but the wind did nothing to stem the heat; matter of fact, it spread it.

Furious with her ankle, Ivory was hard pressed to do better. She was a fighter, and if the medicine woman was trying to punish her for whatever reason, she was not giving an inch.

'You must be burning,' said Ginny in a faraway voice.

It was an absolute furnace.

When big clouds gathered in the horizon, Ivory brightened.

They followed the giant clouds, grey clouds that took rain away with them, and when next Ivory looked at the glaring sky there were just small fluffy clouds dissipating under a fierce red sun.

The water in the gourd around Ginny's neck was gone. Mortality was a statement if not reality. Ivory didn't realise how bad her condition was until Ginny grabbed her from a swoon.

Ivory gladly dropped to the ground under a desert oak that offered little shade, and watched as the medicine woman broke a feathery leaf and crushed it. She offered its sap to Ivory, and it tasted like urine. A blanket of bottle flies pestered Ivory, but none of them touched Ginny.

'Possum oil,' said the medicine woman.

Ivory braved the foul-smelling fat on her skin, and that resolved the bottle flies, but she remained firm on the matter of eating a live grub from the second of Ginny's pouches.

2.

Somewhere along the way, Ivory got her legs.

She and the medicine woman walked and walked, but it wasn't long before Ginny pulled Ivory down to the ground again. Wordlessly, also from the second pouch, Ginny pulled a red kangaroo paw, chewed its petals, spat an apostrophe of the mush into one palm, bent Ivory's knee and rubbed gooey all around the reddened ankle. She rubbed saltbush sap on the blistered toes.

'Why did you choose to become a seer?'

'You do not choose it.'

'How do you know you have the gift?'

'It is not a gift. It is a sacrifice.'

'Where is the rest of your family?'

'To follow the path of the seer, sacrifices must be made.'

'Did you slaughter them?'

Ginny laughed. 'Don't be dramatic. I sacrificed not to have children.'

'I thought it's the gift... the sacrifice... that chooses you.'

Ginny glared at her. 'The childlessness, that's a sacrifice I chose.'

'But how do you know when you have it? The seeing?'

'Sometimes you need a terrible fear to summon your greatest strength.'

In a new wave of chattiness as they renewed their trek, Ginny started pointing things out. 'That crooked old tree? It is a desert oak. Young ones are taller, thinner.'

The telling didn't much distract Ivory from the discomfort of the heat, and the shade of a monstrous boab whose trunk swallowed and regurgitated a sizzle of heat, was wasted on them.

'This one has roots that run kilometres long,' said Ginny. Later she pointed at a tree. 'Black wattle, a good one for the digging stick.' Flora and fauna were at the tip of Ginny's tongue. Methodically she unravelled the desert world: the prickly leaves of a bottlebrush – powerful medicine, good in tea; the distinctive red of a waratah plant – permanent paint. She peeled bark off a honey-myrtle tree and fed Ivory moisture from the trunk. Facing the morning sun, she pointed out a topaz cloud shaped like a crab on the horizon. 'Rain.'

When they found a swamp, Ivory had the intelligence to know they didn't just happen upon it. In the tranquillity of the mud, Ginny made a rough spear from sticks and stones and caught a stingray. Later, she pointed out a berry. '*Gijigiji* berry. Red, soft and luscious like a beautiful woman. And just as poisonous.' She pointed to mangroves in the distance. 'Mozzies, sand flies, crabs and crocs. Mangroves are relatively harmless, save for the milky sap one. It blinds.' Everything in the bush had a purpose, she said.

'Even blinding milk sap?' asked Ivory.

'Cures sting rash.'

They saw snakes (edibles) and turtles (inedibles). Taught by an expert, Ivory watched the cloud peak. Salt breeze brought a refreshing scatter, relief all the way to Wonga, a rural village in black stump country. There they rested in the hospitality of strangers whose eyes never sought those of the seer but whose hospitality was borne with the lightness of a summer breeze. A man, who had been fixing a car that sounded like a gunshot each time he revved it, dropped his tools and drove them – *pough!* – squeezed in the front as the car jumped – *pough!* They drove past gorges, sandstone, shrubbery and corrodes of rugged earth. *Pough!* Despite these regular gunshots, the car hobbled resolutely until it arrived without incident at another rural community where children bounced on a trampoline and women tossed giggling babies in the air and caught them before they dropped. Young lads licked their lips at the prospect of money, but the driver was only visiting an uncle, and waved gleefully after exchanging greetings with the older man, and – *pough!* – the car hopped all the way to Pepper Coona who had abandoned Ivory to the mercy of a seer.

If you look inside medicine woman eye, Ivory remembered the girl's fright, *you die.*

Despite her terror, Pepper agreed to drive Ginny and Ivory to the airport, where they caught a flight to Sydney.

3.

Now in Sydney, the morning had started off cloudy, longitudes of silver and grey in a sky topaz with dawn. A soft fall of rain, dark clouds looming aloft, gave surety of further downpours. A rainstorm was unwelcome yet much needed to revive drought areas in cattle country down west, thought Ivory.

Punter's Grove overlooked the glitz of Dock 72. The dockside with its boulevards and wedding cake houses, mostly white and Victorian, had character. But Punter's Grove carried its own disposition. Dawn traffic cruised along adjacent roads on the shore side of Harbour Bridge. Twinkling headlights dappled windows already bearing titanium-white, orange and purple glamour of glass walled mansions.

Inside Punter's Grove, in the penthouse, a master bedroom still wore a warm glow of opulence: gas heaters, marble margins, mantelpieces in two pack gloss enamel...

Ivory attended the crime scene wrapped up in plastic. She could just see tomorrow's headlines: *Ash Magician Strikes Again!*

The homicide team was already there. She nodded at the senior sergeant, a friendly sort not suited to this type of gruesome. Opposite a granite hearth with a barley twist rail and traditional ram's head poker, victim no. 1 lay on a crimson-spattered bed. He was hands and feet akimbo, bound to chains dangling from the ceiling.

Ivory's colleague, Senior Constable Nick Hogan, arrived late at the scene. 'Hey, Whitey.'

'Where the heck were you?'

'Missed you too.' He looked at her polypropylene gear. 'What's with the overalls?'

'I've got trust issues.'

'Nothing to worry about.' He pointed towards her neckline. 'That stone of yours protects you.'

'Maybe it doesn't.'

He nodded at the homicide team. 'Women not cut out for this?'

'What am I then?'

'One of us. Whatever motivates you to do what you do, I admire it.'

'Quit yapping already. There's a massive crime scene to process.'

He studied the victim and lifted a hand to scratch his very white, very wispy hair. 'Some death wish. Homicide share any thoughts yet?'

Ivory met his powder blues, eyes that sometimes looked almost a pale green. 'Obviously still figuring it out.'

She looked around the room wrapped in semi darkness, lit only by the faint orange glow from an array of ten small candles. More chains, hooks, whips and a hanging rope – noose and all. A pilot cap sat askew on the victim's shoulder. His glitter costume was unevenly torn, the red on its lining different from the spray of crimson around the walls. The width and depth of the blood stains shouted the energy of violence that had occurred in the room.

'Caucasian male. Five foot nine.' Ivory started her prelims. 'Hair dark brown (short clipped),' she spoke to her recorder. 'Puncture marks on the wrist. Lower front teeth missing. Lower abdomen split open. Top of the head blown off.'

There was no need to describe the splatter of blood and brain. Forensics was already on the photo shoot, moving tripods, zooming lenses, varying scale, snapping clips to close-ups. The angles, the measurements, the samples of evidence (multiple booze glasses, semen, etc) appeared to shape a crime. The victim couldn't have secured himself and killed himself. Another of the squad team was collecting DNA: brain matter, hair strands, blood, saliva, soot... There was soot everywhere. Two other officers processed surfaces for latent prints.

Inside a different room with natural light an officer was attending the two female victims. The décor in this room was no less lavish. Raw brickwork with a sandstone mantelpiece enclosed furniture of polished antique oak.

On a nickel stand, or mini table, stood evidence of a party or a sumptuous meal: a roast of barramundi on a silver tray garnished with stuffed tomato; oysters topped with artichoke shavings; an ornament of crisped calamari. Martini goblets rimmed with lipstick. An ice bucket held half a bottle of vintage sparkly. A few paces away on a Persian rug, a silk camisole with lace entangled denim crop jeans in a scrunched heap.

'Victim no. 2.' Ivory spoke to her recorder. 'Olive skinned female, four foot seven. Hair mousy (shoulder length), eyes hazel through slots of an executioner's leather mask (black). Alive, evidence of shock. Ash-like substance on her skin.'

Ivory's gaze moved. 'Victim no. 3. Black skinned female, five foot one. Hair dyed blonde (tousled) with dark highlights. Navy nursemaid uniform – white collar, turn-up cuffs. Also evidence of ash. Presence of frothing at the mouth. Unconscious.'

Eventually emergency services stretchered out both victims, and undertakers removed the body bag under police escort to a windowless van for the coroner's in the CBD.

'Think post mortem will reveal what we don't already know?' asked Nick.

'Clearly with the common denominator of the ash…' Ivory shrugged.

Before long, removal specialists would take over the site. But for now and perhaps for three more days it was still a crime scene on lockdown, and you only had one shot at it before the public contaminated things.

The dust on a glass-topped coffee table had the toxic smell of crack, as did more white dust on the floor, blended with soot. The forensic crew also found bandit pills, translucent chewies and barbiturates.

'Joint is an addict's haven,' said Nick.

Despite the anomalies of a bigger drug cache than normal – usually the victims were plain drunk – the killer's modus operandi fit the Operation Limelight classic.

With the females amped out either from crack or shock, Ivory shook her head. 'What do you bet our dead guy is a twin?'

'I'd bet everything.'

'If our hunch is right, our killer is getting desperate.'

4.

Superintendent Grant Pugley sat concrete at his desk inside HQ.

It was one hell of a weekender, a winter that came along with spits of rain and maudlin weather, and Ivory was not excited about facing her boss. But she did.

'Seen the papers?' he barked.

'Yes, Superintendent.'

'Punters Grove is in the spectacular heart of the metropolis. People who can take you out of a job live there.'

'Yes, Superintendent.'

'You tell me how a murder happens in wind-licked suburbia, rib to rib with the waterfront. Know what kind of security they pay for houses up there?'

'This looks bad.'

'Bad? *Bad?* We're not selling fish here. I need fucking results! Your incompetence to solve these crimes reflects on me, you know. You're putting me in an impossible position. Your incompetence will torpedo me into early retirement with a sheep's arse pension and a grudge the size of a tank. It's not just *my* career on the line. You *do like* your job, don't you?'

'Yes, Superintendent.'

'What do you have to say for your cockup?'

'We're running on a thin budget, sir.'

'Budget?' Pin sharp eyes on his bulldog face. 'Let me reset the fucking bar. When I call you to this office – see those trophies on the shelves? – when I summon you in here, it is *not* for high tea and crustless sandwiches.'

'No, sir.'

'First Somerville, then Eliza Quay, then Baxter, now Punter's Grove.'

'There was one in Newtown and a borderline in Redfern, we're not sure it's the same –'

'They call him the Ash Magician.'

'Sir, we don't know it's a man.'

'And then you think up an ace – a seer.' Thick brow raised. 'Where is this woman now?'

'I –'

'Sitting on my money in a five-star hotel facing Harbour and Bondi Beach where someone is murdered. Palm trees soothing her?'

'Sir, I –'

'Here's your bill.' He pushed forward a sheet. 'And that's a running bill. What's she on? Acupuncture and tennis practice?'

'I'll look into it –'

'Oh, you bloody well will. Look into it. The press has gone wild. This morass of death is sending everything wild. Sydney's in panic. And a seer's your bingo.'

'She listens to spirits –'

'Tell her spirits to listen to your future. Something's coming, and it's not going to be nice. Playtime is over. Issue a press release.'

'We can't, Superintendent, not yet!'

'Full report on my desk. First thing tomorrow. And *I* determine when it's yet.'

5.

'Hey, Whitey.' It was Nick. 'Having fun yet?' He sat on her desk dangling his feet.

'Shut up and follow me.'

There were no creases on his uniform. He was spotless as usual. The first time she met him at a beat, they were not in uniform. It was some drug bust that didn't happen. Pugley had made a few calls, ordered her on the streets in casuals and she found herself lumped, no introductions, with a man wearing powder blue eyes and very white, very wispy hair. He came out of a café with a takeaway cup.

The day was a sizzler, mirages in your eyes everywhere. Bahati called it the mean path of summer, solar radiation on the ground surface every which way. The buildings were sweating, aircons groaning. Glossed windows in high oblong towers blinked at the white sun.

Ivory looked the plain clothes up and down as he approached. 'Know what incognito means?'

'What?' He took a sip.

She pointed at him. 'Not this. You from Melbourne?'

'Why?'

'Two things: What sort of dickhead wears a tie in summer?'

He laughed. 'And two?'

'Who drinks coffee after midday?'

'Trying to drag a free coffee out of me? I can buy you one.'

'Is that an offer?'

He chucked the Styrofoam cup in a bin and stretched his hand. 'Hey, Whitey. My name's Nick.' He had an honest grip, just right: he was not a nutcracker, or a wuss. 'What's the story?'

'Looks like we'll get along,' she said.

The team was assembled in the conference room. Ivory slapped a tablet on Nick's desk. 'You're taking minutes.'

'I think –'

'We're not here to analyse the ins and outs of a duck's bum.'

'Boss!'

'And we're not analysing split peas either. Don't think, just do.'

'Sure thing, Whitey.'

She jabbed him. 'Call me that in private. Here, it's Inspector.'

'Yes, boss.'

She turned to the crew. 'Melvin.'

'No definitive geographical profile. Geological analysis of samples from the victims yields a random pattern. The victims are not related, the killings appear random.'

'Ralph.'

'DNA profiling does not tie the victims, except that all the dead are men, one of twins, murdered in the act of intercourse, after ejaculation. None of the female victims appear to be twins. Everyone covered in bristle ash.'

'Let's brainstorm this.'

After a few minutes of mayhem, sentences became discernible.

'There's nothing medical to explain the survivors' mental state.'

'Is it not natural to conclude that witnessing a horrific crime might induce extreme shock?'

They studied the comprehensive résumés of each crime scene.

Everything in each instance was done by the book. At the end of the brainstorm, they were no better off than at the start.

'There's nothing more to do here,' said Ivory. 'Team dismissed.' To Nick and the laptop: 'Recorded anything yet?'

On the way out, he pressed her shoulder with a friendly hand. 'Chin up, Whitey. Enjoy what you do.'

6.

At Tiffany Hotel, Ivory said, 'There must be some mistake. This is one hell of a bill.' She pointed at the rates. '*Per day?*'

'Honeymoon suite, darling.'

'Keep calling me darling if you want to know hand-to-hand combat.'

'Is that even legal?' the fresh-faced buck at the help desk said.

'Resisting arrest.'

'For what!'

'Thuggery. What the heck's this: Room service special – high fibre diet?'

He cleared his throat. 'The senior constable left instructions to give the seer whatever she asked.'

Eugen Bacon

Ivory rapped once and entered the honeymoon suite of Edwardian style. The cornice was swathed in pastels and gold.

Ginny sat cross-legged, meditating on the floor.

'Pollen of mangle kangaroo paw?' said Ivory without preamble. 'Bottlebrush shoots? Desert peas… Are you mad?'

Ginny was quiet, not looking at her, yet Ivory could hear her. *Greetings to you, too*, said a voice in Ivory's head. Ginny's lips had not moved.

'You eat lizards. What's wrong with a plain eye fillet?'

Stop hovering above me flapping a piece of paper, it is drinking my blood.

'Seriously? We're doing this now?'

Feisty as they come. I forgive your lack of manners. You were orphaned young.

Feeling too deep, too flat, Ivory stared in disbelief at the barren wilderness of the young seer's eyes.

Cold ashes. Words like jaws.

'What?'

That death. Nothing you can do.

Ivory's legs went. She collapsed on a plush couch. 'You win. That's right. Nothing I can do, maybe just a press conference and a resignation before they fire my ass.'

We wait. The voice spoke inside the big pounding of Ivory's head.

'I'm on the clock. You said you would help.'

Charcoal eyes regarded her.

Let us go to Sydney. The buntu has killed again, said the voice in her head. *I remember very clearly, that's what I said.*

Ivory stared at her palms.

Go to the coroner's.

Ivory stared at the medicine woman. 'Sure thing. I'm not going anywhere without some straight answers.'

Ginny Mo'unga did not stir. Her eyes turned inwards, the voice in Ivory's head gone.

7.

Nick's call found her one foot in the car amidst a downpour.

'You've got some explaining –' she began.

'Whitey, you better see this. Coroner's. See you in five.'

'The heck, Nick. You can't just –'

'Seriously, be here,' he said, and the line dulled.

Rivers of lashing rain sluiced the curb. The windscreen danced a loud heartbeat. It took more than five minutes to find parking.

Nick met her at the door. 'It's Pat.'

Ivory remembered the pathology intern. Shy smile. Red head. Only this time she wasn't so shy – she was thrashing about in a seizure, and the men in the room struggling to hold her down. At the far end on a trolley was a covered cadaver.

Sirens.

By the time the emergency crew arrived, Pat had settled. Other than lolling her head, tongue out and dribbling, she was no longer heaving.

'Touched the corpse,' someone said. 'First a trance. Then the seizures.'

Ivory looked about the room. 'Who normally does autopsies?'

'The coroner, but he was double-booked. And the intern, she knows –'

'You idiots!' snapped Ivory. 'No woman should touch the body, or attend suspected *buntu* crime scenes.'

Later, Nick said. 'Inspiration, Whitey?'

'Starting to add up. The Sin Palace man who went gaga. Can we get a medical on him?'

'He's already had a medical. And he's still gaga.'

'I mean medical history. Right from birth.'

'See what I can do.'

8.

Night closed like a fist.

Ivory sat on a step in the privacy of her backyard and gazed at a slope with its patches of rock and sprouts of magnolias. Creams and purples, heart drops and gladiolas bedecked the garden. Once a month, a fellow from *Jim & Spick* stopped by to pull out crawlies and vines. He hoed the soil and fluffed it up, sprayed the garden and shared a cuppa.

She loved the silence of her two-bed; a home of untapped potential off Creek Road. Untapped potential... She smiled wryly. Those were the property agent's words when Ivory made the decision to move out of Bahati's bachie pad and, together, they chose the weatherboard.

She looked at the night and she knew it, the same dusk slippery with secrets that had visited Creek Road yesterday, the day before and all last week. Its moon cast a soft glow on the dancing leaves of the young trees lining the roadside, the neat array of cars positioned outside town houses. A street lamp with a broken light stood sentry like a tall boy with a cleft lip waiting for a change of guard.

She brooded with no makeup, in faded denims and canvas trainers, gazed out into twilight, open to what dreams dusk gave. She was grateful how far she had come since Izett, a little girl with matted hair and all she had in a garbage bag. That was the girl she was as foster home after foster home broke her spirit. How she envied the children with the real parents at the foster homes, their sense of entitlement!

She wondered about her childhood, if at all she could call it that. It was filled with skipping across weeds, thorns and bricks. For other children with real mums and dads, there was no danger field, no price checker. Nothing was poison, worry or toil, everything was food, sleep or play. There was room for today, always today, never tomorrow. Pyjamas rainbowed with life's circus jazzed with the belly laughter of red-nosed clowns waltzing tippy-toed with the tigers one act away from the trick ponies. Skippy all carefree, many cuts from play, still no scars. Come rain, come shine, they didn't need to study the fortune forecast because they were children blessed with golden sand and they could build castles to their whims. They were kings and queens in their households. Everything belonged to them: the mums, the dads, the living rooms, the rainbow mugs, the tellies... even the swings and the rides in the mums' and dads' cars – the window seats. Only the pets she pretended to own, and that was an easy pretend to have because cats and dogs naturally loved her.

Once she outgrew the foster homes, she waitressed here and there, took the odd cleaning job to stay afloat. She was determined never to be a burden any more, never again to feel how the foster families made her feel, and she was doing just fine on her own, independence and all, until a man from the bar in a basement club reminded her that she was nothing. But mild-mannered Bahati came along with his professorship, skin the colour of pale sandalwood and the gaze of a koala that wanted to sleep, and he pulled her from the curb and took her to his home.

With him she never felt a stranger, not for one minute, even when he pushed her from a kiss that came with electricity, she never felt she was a burden. She woke up the next morning in his bed and found him curled in discomfort on the floor, and she insisted he get her a sleeping bag from the Salvos. Instead he got rid of the double single and its fat mattress, bought two futons, and she cohabited with him in his bachie pad until she was ready to move out. When he suggested night school, she suggested enrolling in her new name. Ivory.

'To bury an impossible past,' she said.

'And why Tembo?'

'I've always loved elephants,' she said.

Bahati became parent, sibling, friend and mentor, everything she had yearned for. He was like the mandisa pine, fierce in his protection of her, and she had no doubt he would spit and hump and chase anyone who misunderstood her with twigs and stones. She was keenly infatuated with him, stayed infatuated even when he introduced her to his twin brother, Sam, who was nothing like Bahati, was intently keen on irking Ivory with his flirting and never taking her seriously. Something about him reminded her of the foster dads, and she couldn't help but slash at him with words like a blade. She was too big to lash at people with her fists, Bahati said. How, wondered Ivory, could two people so identical be so light and shade? Bahati also introduced her to his friends, who mostly taught at the university. Friends like Pygo the native elder who had hooked her up with the medicine woman. Not once did Bahati mention a girlfriend, and she was sure he preferred boys until one day in his bachie pad, three years later...

And it was worth the wait. With him it was a dance, unlike other men who grabbed, snatched and tore. Bahati offered a dance with its rise and falls, one... two, three. One... two, three. Unusual, daring, always safe, it was a weightless fall. No wonder she dreamt about him in that wonderful sleep on kangaroo skin inside the red mud hut when the girl absconded, and the medicine woman extended her hospitality, and Ivory wafted in and out of clouds of sleep filled with waterfalls bursting in arcs and sweet Bahati holding out a glass of soda and rum.

9.

Windscreen dazzle torched the backyard. The gleam swept round the fence, and Bahati's 4WD parked at the front. His tall, lean frame fell out of the car together with an excitable fifty-pounder.

'Hello you,' he said.

'Hey.'

Slobber was a fawn boxer with a black head and muzzle, a naturally muscular and sturdy dog that was first mad keen on licking Ivory's face and then he did a wild dog thing cutting diagonals across the yard. He was Bahati's mid-life crisis when Ivory chose to find a pad of her own. Men on transition generally bought a Porsche or did some random thing like learn to fly a plane – Bahati went to a shelter and adopted a strong-legged dog.

'What brings you to Creek Road?' Ivory said. Her face was wet still with the dog's saliva.

'Those emerald eyes and perhaps a soda and rum.'

They laughed.

'Look, I'll make you dinner.' He pulled groceries from the car. She helped him as Slobber loped and galloped, barked at their heels, insane with joy – or was it jealousy?

'You have him all the time,' said Ivory. 'My turn now, hey?'

'Play nice,' said Bahati.

She watched as he sizzled up chicken thigh fillets on the hob. She tried to be helpful, peel the pumpkin, but he wouldn't have any of it. So she leaned by the sink and talked as he worked.

'Done teaching your brilliant students, Professor?'

'The buggers question everything, doesn't make them brilliant.'

'Emotion is twenty-four percent stronger than logic. And you are the gentry-speaking, highly intelligent one who hates to be challenged.'

'That's hard to defend. You are a dream killer, my girl.'

She ruffled his curls. 'Let's get you that soda and rum.'

He cubed the pumpkin and garnished it with pine nuts, served it up with a creamy risotto with pesto and blistered tomatoes.

He let her do the dishes, not much work.

'Yep, we're dishwasher friendly,' she said. She arrayed spoons, knives and plates efficiently, the smaller pots – Bahati used heaps of pots cooking – and turned the device to an eco wash. She hand-scoured the bigger pans.

He was rubbing Slobber on the steps, the dog's tail wag wagging.

'More soda?'

'Sure thing.'

They sipped drinks and watched Slobber, fully committed to another mad dog thing.

They sat on the porch.

'Ginny helping you on that murder?'

'Nick might help me – he's researching on Sin Palace. Ginny? She's something else.'

'Track down the seer, is all I said. You had to go and bring her back with you.'

'Don't push it, Sweet Cheeks. I am no less the cynic.'

'Be convinced and see what happens.'

'She is running away from me. Logic is running away from me. Case is running.'

'It's all a state of mind. Focus, application. You need to find rhythm.'

'Now my boyfriend is talking like a seer.'

'Look outside,' he said. 'See the mist?'

'What mist?'

'It's there, right there. It's the mist, bleeding over the mundane, offering mass classes for culprits of mundane conversation to unlearn bad phrasing and ingenuine compliments pregnant with unsaid malice coerced into the kind of flirting that may inhabit a deceased's estate.' He fondled her fingers. 'As the mist flows like a network of trains into your veins, like a bare toed investor spilling with altruism, finally it reaches your atrium and you smile at the lollipop man crossing you over to the other side of the street, and you say, *How are you tracking?* And you look at the middle-aged woman at the bus stop and give her a compliment on her poise. *Don't break too many hearts*, you say.' He looked at her. 'It's the mist, calculating, unapologetic, racing its platelets all over you. It reshapes the way you understand yourself and, like a policeman reciting the rights, it's not a choice.'

'So academic. Please tell me you read that in a book somewhere. Bahati, you're scaring me.'

'All I'm saying… is focus.'

Slobber lay panting at their feet, gazed wistfully under a sky staggered with white stars.

10.

He guided her yoga on a carpet.

'Tantra embraces all forms of expression,' he said. 'Eating, drinking, smelling and loving.'

She inhaled, drew her torso forward and parallel to the floor. He guided the spread of her hands.

'Tantra is a sacred art that raises inner energy to a mystical state,' he said.

She turned her toes, exhaled and lifted her knees from the floor.

'You are interfaced to a cosmic solidarity of human souls.'

She held her hips level for 30 seconds.

'Tantra purifies body and mind, masters them to awaken the power of the psychic.'

She brought her big toes together and sat on her heels.

'You are a student of life.'

She folded to a resting pose, a child in the womb.

'Focus your energy,' he said, 'to your mind, soul and spirit.'

She went on all fours, knees below her hips.

'You are a goddess,' his voice was full of husk. 'Your body is a temple of divinity.'

He coloured her world and, together, they explored a place full of dew and honey.

11.

Later, much later, she murmured in his arms. 'Tell me the story.'

'Again?'

'Tell me.'

He cradled her close. 'Once upon a time before the roll of years, of seasons replacing seasons, of wind pushing rain drenching sun bringing light, there lived a man on Earth. He was tall as a mandisa pine, an outcast who fell in love with a chief's daughter.'

'She was a twin.'

'Yes, Madam Clever. And they spoke of her beauty far and wide. One black night, he stole into chief's compound, mistook one of the chief's wives' for his daughter. The marksmen aimed and he caught fire. He died by fire for his blunder.'

'But he didn't die – his souls separated.'

'As for Dotto, his love –'

'She killed herself with root poison.'

Bahati paused. 'And so, dear heart, you do know the story. Then why, oh why...'

'Just tell it, Willie.'

'As one soul travelled the spirit world to find Dotto, the other stayed trapped inside a calabash in a sacred place. And the Valley of Dreams was enraged at the pointless death of a man whose only crime was to love a twin, and it soared to the galaxies.'

'And became a world of a new species of ivory eyes and purple hair', said Ivory. 'And in this world there lived two spirited boys. They were Ku and Doh, who were wild as the sea and like as corn.'

'Folk called them the cheeta boy twins. Not only did they run faster than wind, like the cheeta animal in this part of the universe, they were like as cheeta peapods – vegetables that grew in the far corner of the Valley of Dreams.'

'But before the boys there was a valley, ancient terra firma that once long ago ruptured its roots from Earth and elevated itself in an arc,' said Ivory. 'It soared to a place beyond two asteroid belts, a space within the moon's orbit where it joined a galaxy of independents where stars altered shape and became triangles, then petals, then diamonds... Octagonal. Hexagonal. Oval. Ringed. And finally back to star shape.'

'You're going backwards – what happened to keep the plot moving?'

'Just tell it, Willie,' said Ivory.

'So there in the Valley of Dreams, a world that's light years from Earth, the boy twins Ku and Doh were full of mischief.

They unsettled the spirit buried in the calabash, and it smelled like how they describe demons.'

'VOOPFH!'

'That was the sound the beast made when it rose from the rib of a calabash the boys kicked in the hushed grounds of a sacred place.'

'*Voopfh!*' cried Ivory.

'Frightened of what they had unleashed, the boys fell to the ground, elbows on heads, and cried in tongues to the gods of the Great Chief Goanna to take pity on them.' Bahati looked at Ivory. 'And only a seer can put it right, guide them all to the place of dreams.'

'Time before time.'

Seven: The X and Y Genome

1.

Back in the office, Nick had garnered impressive paperwork. He had a medical report, a psychiatric report and a deductive report, all on the Sin Palace survivor.

'Born Gideon Sumner, 27 February 1968. Kilwa. Father was a dominating Presby, cyclone persona, once won a 400m medal in State Championships. Fathered twelve children, mostly girls, one boy. Mother was a housewife, tried her hand at a flower shop, a bakery, a women's club. The caravan that housed them was cramping, before they moved to a wood cabin, then a red-roofed chalet with a garden.'

'And all that's helping me solve this crime how?' asked Ivory.

'A few domestic incidents, and the boy – Gideon – hated sport, had no interest in girls, except the dresses they wore. Turned out he was born dual sexed, the parents had insisted on the surgery that had physically made him a boy, but he did possess an extra X chromosome.'

'*Klinefelter's* syndrome. Might explain why his symptoms were like the women's.'

2.

At Tiffany Hotel, she waited an hour for Ginny because the medicine woman had left instructions not to be disturbed and was not picking up the reception call. Inside the honeymoon suit, the seer smelt of honeysuckle and wood. She sat in meditation, commanded that Ivory assume the same cross-leggedness and face a pattern of pebbles, kangaroo paw and twigs on the carpet.

Curtains blew wild, although there was no wind.

'Ginny –'

'Keep the silence,' said a voice inside a voice, almost clinical.

Communing with the seer when she was in this state was self-contained and dangerous. It was an act that lay in shadows, eyeing invisible beasts that sang with echo. The day tucked itself and closed its eyes from somewhere beyond. It was like being in a tiny enclosed cube that was sound proofed and inside a bigger cube, also insulated from the world, and inside box after box. It was like the pieces of a nesting doll of increasing size placed one outside another, only these were boxes floating like insignificant specks of dust in space. And Ivory was inside with the dirge of her breath, trapped within cubes, pounding, pounding with her fists and nobody could hear her.

And so Ivory sat through the wisdom of stones to a soothing wind in unscripted worlds until the seer's eyes were no longer inward drawn, and the drapes were still.

'Let us have tea,' Ginny said. She unwrapped from the floor and ordered room service.

They sat at the table sipping tea from porcelain cups, nibbling lettuce encrusted in golden crusts, swallowing queen cakes and croquettes. At the back of her mind, Ivory tried to figure out what mood to assume but, before inspiration could reach her, the seer tilted her head, brushed Ivory's gaze with unreadable medicine woman eyes and spoke with her mind.

It is a sex jini.

'A what?'

It is attracted by lust, the act of intercourse.

'How do we stop it?'

Soon. It was a whisper. *We're going on a journey.*

Coal eyes drew her like magnets, eyes that knew intimate things about her.

Your father, he is happy with who you are.

Ivory numbed.

He is sorry your mother was too fragile for something as momentous as you.

Ivory stared at the seer in steep silence.

He asked the dingos to guide your mother when she ran away from him, and the gods of our forefathers to deliver you to the missionaries. He is sorry about the rest, everything else that happened, but he spoke to the wind that brought Bahati to you.

'Tell me about the journey,' Ivory said in a whisper.

'For now, we wait.'

'Right here?'

'Find Bahati. The time is near.'

3.

Ivory phoned Bahati, got his voicemail. She tried his brother Sam's number, and was trying to leave a message when Sam called back.

'I was feeling a bit off today until you called,' he said.

'Good, touched by an angel. Are you sober right now?'

'I'm fair dinkum, bloody oath, I've been drinking since I was in a pram.'

'Explains much. Now get serious.'

'Damn. What a knockout.'

'Heard from Bahati?' she asked.

'No. But there's a double on standby. At your service, my lady.'

'Sam, not in the mood.' A mallet was pounding her forehead. 'Get Bahati to call me if you speak to him first?'

4.

Hocking Grove stood on the road to Kew at the corner of Marble St and Nichols St, two blocks from a riverside drive. Rain murmur was lost on a silhouette in the dark alleyway, a shadow removed from the glare of street light several metres up the road. Synthetic glass of a tram stop sheltered the hooded watcher from incessant drizzle. Shower covered distance from the hard plastic shield to a 50s townhouse with brick veneer, an original two-level building with attic extension in different tint forming a lone garret. Similar detached townhouses, without extensions, stood in rows along the roadside.

The watcher fumbled in his pockets and pulled out a cigarette stick separated at some point from the rest of its pack, crushed by a pseudo-flat lighter inside the same pocket. He sparked the nicotine, tucked it between his lips. He smoked quick puffs, hands shaking. Each drag animated the glow on the outer tip, baby swirls of his smoke swelling into billows. He exhaled white horns, and waited.

The night was nippy, its cold sweeping across the city, a promise of high wind and much rain in the coming overnight downpour. But the smoke was good. It lifted chill from the folds in his clothes and warmed his skin. However, it reduced to a miniature butt too soon. He crushed it underfoot and dug into his pocket for another – his last.

Moments before he sparked, tube lights blinked behind curtains in the upper level of a townhouse. He paused. The lights snapped off. Holding his breath, he waited. Slowly, a second glow. Not flickering, nothing like television might make; this one steadied. Nerves frazzled, he lit the cigarette. Swift erratic puffs. As he dragged, he saw her at the window. Right there on the second level.

She stood waist up behind drapes that swayed. The gleam in the room deepened to a red hue. Inside it, almost in slow motion, the woman lifted a hand to her neck. She began stroking her throat in seductive mode. Fingers moved downwards to the base of her blouse's neckline crested on her breasts. She unbuttoned the top.

His smoke became less erratic, more in control. Deep, long pulls on the stick in his mouth, a slow exhale from the side of his lip. A calmer drip! drip! drip! from the eaves of the protector joined the pitter patter of rain around him. A clap of thunder chased his thoughts back to the window, to the outline of the stripping female.

Her hand slipped out of a sleeve. His eyes followed the loosened top sliding off the other arm. She turned her back on him. Reaching behind, she unclasped a bra, swished it to and fro, acting out the swing, then dropped the skimpy piece.

Distant car wheels splashed. Rain sang overhead.

She stood semi-naked behind the drapes, posing for him. Her thumb hooked coyly in her waistband. She paused. Then, in controlled movement, she bent and peeled her stockings. He imagined the scent of her lingerie, the velvet of her skin, the cream of her flesh. She tantalised him, toyed with his need. She licked one hand from inside elbow to fingertip, ran wet palms through her hair, fingers outstretched, sat on the sill, elbow out, hand to her waist like a lingerie model.

And then she drew the curtain. Now he saw her, not behind gauze. A shaft of lightning dazzled her face. Dark sprawling hair fell to her waist. She sat totally with possession but without soul. The fine angle of her jaw; the lean elongation of her neck; the proportion of her bust pushed out between her breasts, their pointed tips, the rise and fall of her chest; the map of her ribs to her stomach to the swell of her thighs; the robustness of her rounded hips, the naked art of her body...

And yet.... something lacked. Her pose seemed adopted for him. Perhaps it was the ensemble of her face or her eyes that held no fire or passion. She was the most perfect creature he had ever seen, in an arctic sort of way, striking yet cold as frost.

A man appeared from one the end of the window. The woman paused a moment and then stood. Slowly, she went out of view. The lustrous gleam of her hair vanished last. Pitter! patter! pitter! patter! drip! drip! drip!

The hooded watcher tossed the glowing stick to drenched ground. And, although it sizzled and died inside a thin but growing puddle, he poised a deliberate foot and crushed it.

5.

Inside another part of Sydney, the same pitter patter of light rain and a white glimmer of starlight caught the roof of the weatherboard house in Creek Road.

Ivory couldn't explain to Bahati her frantic search of him earlier. But he was here now, and that was all that mattered.

He lay face up atop the bed, hands at the back of his head. 'Medicine Woman said all that?'

'Your father is happy with who you are – present tense.'

'All that from her bones?'

'Pebbles, kangaroo paw and twigs on the carpet.' Ivory pressed her chin against the pillow. 'I wanted to hate her. But something about the way she spoke, reaching my mind with her silence… Her words were not the hocus pocus of a hallucinating woman.' She looked at him. 'She said it was no accident you found me that night.'

'Who ever said it was an accident?' He smoothed her hair. 'Sleep now. Work tomorrow.'

He held her in the crook of his arm, their bodies perfectly moulded, and she fell into a light and troubled sleep.

6.

High-pitched ringing burst the silence of her dreams, throttled what promise they carried. Waves of monochrome sliced behind her eyes. She jumped, startled, and blinked sleep from her eyes.

She groped for her phone on the bedside table and it throbbed out of reach, wailing like a banshee. She cursed, pushed herself forward and snapped the alarm silent.

Bahati was nowhere.

She pulled up the honeycomb window shade, a mesh of bamboo, reed and white grass, and spread even light, lots of it, into the room. Brooding, she stared out the window, the swathe of morning sun out in the still wet street.

She listened to the low hum of traffic, periodic honks and the metallic *clong!* of a tram. Finally, she allowed herself the smouldering blast of a shower, a creamy lather of cedar and moss conditioner and a brisk towelling. She wore Glow Signature, generous with it on her neck, armpits and back of the knees.

Downstairs, she pulled the blinds in the south facing living room, opened double hung gliders overlooking the portico and cranked open the kitchen window. Bahati's car was there.

She twiddled with a temperamental toaster that charred bread on whim. She was scraping a blackened slice with a table knife when she caught sight of Bahati from the casement window above the sink.

Loof! came Slobber's jolly bark. He tumbled, ears flattened, tongue hanging, and threw himself across the garden.

The sun lit Bahati's curls. He saw her by the window. She waved. The silent, wistful, brooding she had felt earlier slipped.

They were eating breakfast – he made new toast and some scrambled eggs – when the phone rang.

'Hey Whitey.' It was Nick Hogan.

7.

Ivory met him at HQ.

'What's this?'

'A disaster.'

She ruminated over the facts of the new killings as they turned off the freeway to the main drag of a quiet suburb. Past black gates, white gates, yellow gates, green gates. And trees. Lime trees, loquat trees, guava trees, leafy trees. Fence after fence after fence. Metal gates, wooden gates, no gates... The next neighbourhood had more buzz: a service station, a news agency, a fish & chips shop already open, a community tennis court, a dental clinic...

The day had lost its best weather. People bustled in and out of shops and buildings.

They turned into Riverside Drive then Hocking Grove. Parked outside a detached house ringed with yellow police tape; a townhouse with brick veneer, secure parking and attic extension in contrasting brick. A rotating sprinkler was on full blast in the landscaped garden, unusual since it had rained the night before.

Along a wet footpath, a side door was wide open and intact. A window out the back had been jerried open, said the senior sergeant.

Three paintings in an open living room: one of virginal fruit, another of a comfortably rotund chef sweating into a hand whipped mix, and finally an oil paint of a black and white piglet sitting on a doorstep. Soft pastel wall shade and chrome-capped tube lights achieved a European look.

More paintings draped the bedroom on the second level. There were wall hangings of dazed storks, flying storks, storks carrying twigs... Most were splashed with blood, a trail that led to and from the bedroom where a dead man lay with multiple knife wounds and a bashed-in head. White brain matter was splashed on a red and white table lamp by the bedside. And on the paintings.

The woman was naked, gagged, in the bathtub. She gazed without sight at a boy leading an ebony pony on the blood-splashed wall. She had been knifed multiple times, and a chunk of her buttock was gone.

Covered in cellophane head to toe, Ivory was nonetheless careful to avoid any ash – not that there was any in sight. This was not an Operation Limelight case.

8.

They found a witness, the neighbour, same one who called the police.

'Dancing naked by the window, that's right, danced for the real devil himself,' the woman said. 'First time I saw him, the man that watched her from the street all the time, I knew he was no good.'

'Tell me about the man.'

'Stood right there by the bus stop, smoke after smoke.'

'Can you describe him?'

'Tall man with a hood.'

'Was he Caucasian?'

'Black, red, yellow – how the hell would I know? The streetlights don't shine that good.'

They found cigarette butts by the bus stop, a bloodied kitchen knife stuck in a hedge three houses away.

24 hours later, DNA came back with a match. One Rainer Daemon, recently paroled.

Didn't take long to apprehend him where he was house-sitting a cousin's pad. They found the piece of the woman's buttock in clingwrap inside the fridge.

9.

It was not a buntu killing but the press ran with it anyhow.

Magician's Apostle In Hocking Grove Slaying.

NEW SOUTH WALES – A man arrested for the Hocking Grove slaying of a man and his wife is to appear in court tomorrow. Authorities refuse to confirm that Rainer Daemon is a sworn apostle of The Magician who has been terrorising… The Magician himself is still at large…

'Speculation. Gossip. Innuendo!' barked Superintendent Pugley. 'Fix this!'

10.

Just when things couldn't get any worse, the buntu killed again.

The mall lit like a beacon in the early evening. A street away, 1065 Surrey Crescent was inside a renovated building, south wing, tenth floor. It was not a penthouse. Inside, a fierce noise of drilling. A hallway smudged with grease led into an apartment that carried the look of a weatherboard house but the wooden surface was worn.

Though the house was spacious, it was also cluttered. Once an epitome of finery, perhaps a lover's dream, now it needed a good clean and an overhaul. Windows misted over. Mantels peeled in paint. A wobbly door frame with tattered varnish led to a capable kitchen begrimed with dust, smoke and oil. Dead flies floated on goop in the sink, next to a beleaguered, embattled, avocado green casserole pot.

A flight of wooden steps, rough grained, led to an elevated living area with shifting floors. The homicide team was already at the scene. An officer was attending the female victim, who sat on a couch near an ornate fireplace fallen to run. The victim was a small woman with delicate features, the face of a model. She was looking at a television with snow lines, the blankness in her gaze suggestive of buntu-effect trademarks.

The first bedroom was empty, save for dirty socks under a bed, cigarette butts, empty beer cans, undies scattered across the stained, aged thing that was once a carpet. Three girls in pale blue tunics and red ties personalised a dog-eared calendar of three years ago. The window faced the backyard of a primary school and a new residential development.

The dead man was fully dismembered. Almost an art, irreversible.

11.

It was close to 9 pm when Bahati arrived at her place. He came with a bottle.

The sight of him, not just the vintage red, lifted her mood blackened by needless death.

'I'll stay the night,' he offered.

'Where's Slobber?'

'There's Sam. But I'm more worried about my brother in the house without a chaperon than I am about my dog.'

Their love making was mystical, almost sacred. Tantra. It was a sacred art that raised Ivory to the state of a goddess, her body a temple. Guiding her in the art of conscious loving, he took her to a place where nothing was forbidden, everything spontaneous, meditative. He prolonged her pleasure, channelling their union to a moment of perfect harmony. But her cry, capturing her own pinnacle of Tantra, was alone.

She looked at Bahati. His face, the grimace on it was not of impossible sweetness, but of fear. Something was wrong.

'You must not panic.' He squeezed her hand.

She followed his gaze beyond her shoulder. A sway of drapes. An ashy creature in the shape of a man, a killing machine from the monstrosity of it.

She remembered Ginny's words: It is a sex jini. *It is attracted by lust, the act of intercourse.*

The beast lunged.

A torch of agony blazed Bahati's face. He closed his eyes, convulsing. Ivory opened her mouth to scream, but no sound came. Her amulet glowed, warmed against her skin.

She felt herself slip away. She could not move. She was paralysed.

Eight: Inter-Galactic Odyssey

1.

First she was freefalling, limbs all over, into a chasm. Then the nothingness begun to spin, a twizzle of incessant swirl that transformed into eddies of spiteful wind, a whirlwind that whipped and gobbled. Ivory tumbled inside the pulsing white that alternated with strident black. Last she remembered she was with Bahati, her hands and legs refusing to move.

She caught glimpses of the medicine woman catapulting in and out of the avalanche, transforming in shade from ebony to dazzle, no greys. Suddenly, they were together in naked space, flying like swallows, soaring side by side. Even as they glided, Ginny Mo'unga stretched out a hand. Ivory threw herself toward it but could not reach to clasp it. It was Ginny who found her. Together they pitched into rolling surf. Though their hands stayed clutched, distance stood between them like an invisible bridge that paid no attention to proximity of touch.

And then the distance widened, and Ivory lost Ginny's clasp. She panicked, but a new whirlpool swallowed her cry as she tumbled into a swell of scent that was light amber in colour. It stimulated all her senses and the smell bore a medium sweetness, a blend of nutty and caramel. She felt dizzy. She tried to focus her motion but, just then, an elbow struck her rib, a foot clipped her heel. It was Ginny, her shawl billowed, limbs akimbo. A new wind swallowed her whole and, just like that, the medicine woman was gone.

Ivory fired forward in a compact line. Flip, triple flip, forward burst. Time hung. Time spun. An air stream slapped her face. Solidarity with environment. Suddenly she was wind, soaring effortlessly. Then *whirr!* And the grace was lost. She started falling, tumbling in ungraceful loops, the whir in sync with the beat of her heart that pounded in her ears. Powerless to change what was happening, Ivory could not hold back a cry as she broke from an edge or a cliff or the crown of a hill, and catapulted face down into a labyrinth.

A sudden grip on her elbow, a very calming grip, broke her fall. It was Ginny.

Ivory tumbled with a shout of joy into the medicine woman, clung to her like a pillow, until the quivering inside calmed and the swirl fell away, away... Now there was skylight, an elongated purple cloud on the horizon, microgravity, a new cosmos, a borderless world that was also multidimensional. You turned and the world moved with you, different angles catching your eye with pulsing depth.

Together, inside muted wind, they soared through an endless energy field that pushed and pulled, high, higher, above a crag, into a burst of song. The wings of a bird, one that resembled a golden figbird, flapped at Ivory's face. A wisp of blue under-wing, a yellow tail whistling ahead, and the bird sailed out of reach.

The second break of clasp came as they veered towards an emerald river. White rays of light danced across the water's face, casting shimmer in circular ripples, outlying modular waves. And then Ivory was in a different vortex. Alone. Dim light touched

93

her head and the miasma, churning like a vicious sea, swallowed her whole.

2.

Wherever trouble lurked there were Ku and Doh, the pea-eyed twins. Trapped in childhood, wrapped in mischief, they were at it again, painting Mama Pebble's floor with coloured clay. Spatters of crimson joined wild streaks of green and yellow across ancient walls.

Inside her madness, Mama Pebble understood the boys' hive of mischief but was still annoyed by it. She swept them out of the hut in a rain of twigs. The twins, madly giggling, raced to the far corner of their play space, the sacred place, where a buntu had once risen from the belly of a calabash.

Here they tumbled and flipped, their laughter bringing life to muted land. Ku boasted fine motor skills. Doh boasted speed. In a tremendous display of finger and toe combination, Ku looped and catapulted. Doh watched with doleful eye and then sprinted, leapt and knocked his twin down with a fist. But Ku was also the stronger of the two. A tumble to the ground, Doh made a brave fight but Ku pummelled him down twice. Doh came back in a head butt that Ku deflected with a casual elbow. Doh tossed a punch. Ku stepped aside, his fist more concerted, and Doh crumpled to the ground clutching his belly.

'Yous not my friend.'

'I yous twin. Friend don't matter.'

'Face like possum!'

'And it bother me?'

'Hah didgly didgly hah! I not be yous friend.'

'Yous twin forever and ever.'

They were still arguing when a fiery ball tumbled from the sky to the fields beyond what was once hallowed ground, a place where cheeta peas grew.

Ku and Doh abandoned their fight and recalled a beast that had risen, not from the sky but from the rib of a calabash. A demon that devoured the sun and brought brief darkness to their eyes. A creature whose dust took Mama Pebble's mind. Sometimes, in the past, at new moon, they had caught glimpse of that same beast in an overhead blast, a streak of fireball that lit the sky and sped in high-decibel roar beyond the boys' view to a world out yonder.

Now, in a split second, it was back.

They stood in silence, side by side, hands touching, altogether afraid and intrigued by the lustre in the sky. They stared at each other in a spell that seemed to last a lifetime.

Curiosity overcame fright. A nudge of elbows, a smoulder of investigation in their blood, and they charged after the whirring thing that had split the clouds and was now arrowed aground. It looked different from the ash beast, they knew. And so they guessed:

'Is a bird!'

'A ball!'

'A spear!'

'A buntu!'

3.

Ivory hurled bottom-first from the monstrous lip of chaos, an endless yawn that lunged at her rather than swallowed. Now clouds parted to spit her out, and closed. She tumbled into the fringe of a laughing field that grew hushed. Her landing into the silence was loud, like a mighty blast, and it commanded an upward shoot of compact soil. As she connected with the ground, a surge of pain shot up her hip. Impact flung her body so that she lay in a sprawl, face up, facing the heavens.

Or was it Earth?

The fall dizzied her. She couldn't feel her fingers or toes, and was quite sure she had blown her back, if not all elbows and full knees. She lay on the ground, afraid to move. Grey swam in her vision, fog filled her head. Was she dead, crippled or simply shocked? Even as she pondered, the grey inside her head transformed to coffee and then indigo. Ah wait. Slowly.

Slowly vision came in starts. Red dots... a touch of rainbow off the corners of her eyes... and then orange. When a twinge sparked her calf, she twitched a foot and then wriggled her toes in relief. Her fingers moved. Finally, she lifted on elbows. A soft wind blew the tips of her hair. She turned her head, brow furrowed, and blinked at a kaleidoscope of flowers. The blush of petals ranged in spectrum and sprouted from a sprawl of creepy grass hued reddish brown like port wine. It resembled the wilderness country's spinifex.

She understood all at once: the medicine woman had managed, somehow, to transport them through a portal into a parallel world. But where the heck was Ginny? Hopefully, somewhere in a different perching ground, right here in this amazing place. Ivory took it in, the strange world, and was dazed by it. She fell back again to spreading grass in a sprawl, face up, and studied white triangular stars and a banana moon whose lunar glow shone ever so bright in broad daylight – for there was the sun also in full shine.

As her eyes oriented fully to this world, a world almost cartoon, a world of relentless tint purely a sight to see, she began to isolate flowers. First she picked off scattered heads of purple and white anemones. And then many heads of kangaroo paw. Specks of vibrant azaleas brushed alongside white lilies with remarkable pointers. Predominant ginger on the grassy plain reminded her of Orange Crater, home of Ginny, the medicine woman. But here the orange, when it was orange, was deep, unbreakable. The world looked like it couldn't possibly exist. But it did. Exist.

Body restored, sight renewed, she scanned the new world with a keen eye. The land was first splashed with carroty and rich. Just then, it changed its colour to soft lime. Ivory contemplated it, and realised it was the sun overhead that was changing. It took on a new colour every few moments because, even as she puzzled on the spectacle, it went florid. The triangle stars and banana moon stared down at her bafflement.

Flower heads aground blushed inside the rainbow and rolled across an expanse stippled with an even scatter of trees, blue leaves swaying inside this colour-splattered world. More trees, she saw, trees that were perhaps more like stumps, two of them, and they were moving. They were headed her way and waving branches.

As they approached, Ivory realised they were not stampeding trees or stumps but two half-naked boys with lilac hair chasing in her direction. They tumbled, absolutely soaring, lifting a small cloud of crimson dust. Beyond their racing, in the outer fringe of the now auburn meadow, a smoking hut stood oddly in the horizon, and then nothing more for miles, miles around it.

It was a new world, a fantastic world that had boys or little men, and a smoking shack.

She lay back, face up on the ground.

4.

The twins pondered the new arrival safely, from a distance. It lay face up, limbs sprawled.

The thing looked like them, perhaps more like Mama Pebble in height and skin tone, but then the resemblance ended. Its head was ink black with a hint of blue, not purple. It was cloaked funny, not ha-ha, and it smelt funny, also not ha-ha, just like a strange flower.

It had split the sky and tumbled from it. It was a buntu, but unlike the first. It was a lost spirit that did not smell of soot or sprinkle cinders, and it was not forming and deforming like a smoke or a swarm of bees. It had a skin like Mama Pebble's, not red or blue or inky black as they might have imagined of a strange being, but olive in shade like their own skin. But why, surely, why was a buntu here with them again?

They searched its face for evil or remorse – one of its kind had done something terrible to Mama Pebble – but there was no remorse. They waited for its rage, akin to what they had witnessed of the calabash beast that travelled the worlds, but there was no rage. In fact, this buntu was just scattered on the grass, hair spread on the ground, arms and feet akimbo, and it was looking back at them.

5.

The shock of seeing the twins was more startling than her landing. Outwardly, Ivory did not react to their approach and now they were peering at her with pale eyes. Curious, half-afraid and children as they seemed, who knew what they were? Or could do?

Lying there, stilled by startle, she pondered death and again wondered if she were in it. Were the twins holograms of St Peter or Lucifer himself? They had no horns; that was a good thing. But they were purple haired, and their eyes held no pupils.

As they drew nearer, considering her as if she, not they, were extra-terrestrial, she looked back at them. She disliked children, or was cautious with them, based on her experience with the children of the foster dads and mums with their entitlement and spite and cruelty. Those children's curiosity had been of a mean kind, the kind that sizzled the hair off a pet dog's snout, or bashed a kitten to a brick wall, or assessed to see if darker skin felt pain. Such curiosity had led two brothers to experiment on her soles with their dad's cigarette lighter. That was before they tried to take her amulet and it burnt their hands. They left her alone after that, in a rush, so they didn't see the amulet shine brightly and heal her almost immediately.

But these boys in the fantasy world had a different kind of curiosity. They sized her this way and that, creeping around her like sprites, all the time keeping an even circumference.

They began asking questions, speaking in nasal voices in a language she could partially understand.

'Who yous?'

'Where yous come from?'

'Why yous fly like fire in sky?'

'Yous witch?'

They touched her, at first gently, cried out and sprang back at the feel of her clothing. But they returned, and slowly felt her skin, pulled and pinched it. Ivory shut her eyes. Her head ached. Momentary craving for coffee – of all things she yearned a double espresso – swept through her. The grass was khaki-coloured now, soft as silk.

Ivory dug elbows to the ground and sat up.

They fled.

But again they approached. One held a stick poised. The other steadied a sling. Ivory just looked at them. The weapons lowered. Before long, curious hands touched her hair. Eyes without pupils sought hers.

'What yous?'

'Where coming?'

'Why heres?'

Who, why, when, where? Almost frantic their questioning, their wide-eyed curiosity was the insatiable kind of children. She decided they *were* children. She didn't respond to their questioning, she didn't know why she didn't simply answer them, but she was stubborn that way, or perhaps she was still taking it all in.

They ran from one side of her to the other, leapt from head to sandal, examining. Little hands scoped her turtleneck, followed the pattern of her sandals. They sniffed the Glow Signature on her neck and armpits. Before they could prize it, she stopped them from pulling the ring off her finger, a gift from Bahati whose smile was a pulse to her heart, Bahati who was now pregnant with a buntu, perhaps he was already dead.

Bahati, with his philosophy, he would have known what to do with these boys.

One boy sat on her lap, amazing at her eyes, almost poking fingers into them.

She pushed him away and struggled to her feet.

'Yous buntu woman?'

'Yous no roaring.'

'Where be buntu?'

As nothing halted their questions, and she didn't really have answers, she asked her own.

'Who the hell are you?'

'Me Ku.'

'Me Doh.'

They stood chubby and potbellied, but their faces carried the wisdom of something ancient. And their eyes, those eyes... So full of mischief.

'Why yous eyes colour a grass?' Ku was asking. Or was it Doh?

'Why yous wear earth on yous mouth?'

'What place is this?'

'Valley a Dream,' said Ku. Or was it Doh?

When she tried touching them, they backed away. It didn't matter, really. What mattered was that the boys understood her language. Valley a Dream? Sounded familiar. She wanted to ask more questions, about their eyes, were they always that pale and what had happened to their pupils? About their hair, what dye made such glittering amethyst despite the dusk? But she was hungry, and impatient, and that smoking hut in the distance was as good a prospect as any of getting food.

She began her walk towards the smoke, and the boys yapped alongside her, bombarding her with curiosity.

6.

Bhouff!

That was the sound Ginny Mo'unga made when she connected with the ground. She fell from the sky and landed somewhere between Ivory, the twins and the shack. Ground trembled as she bobbed and skidded along the grass now cloaked with a fog that greyed the air for several minutes before it swelled into a swift shower of rain. A gust of wind pushed the grey mist, racing it away as fast as it had descended, leaving no wetness behind.

When fog fully lifted, Ivory saw the boys lying on the ground, heads tucked inside their arms. Gently she pulled them to their feet, first one and then the other. Their eyes shifted from the sky to the space where Ginny lay.

'Don't be afraid,' Ivory said. She walked towards the tartan shawl and wondered how the heck Ginny hadn't lost it in the whirlwind. The purple-haired twins reached the medicine woman first.

'Ginny.' Ivory bent over the medicine woman, and said her name again.

A slow stirring, and then Ginny swept the shawl from her face. Ivory helped her to her feet. 'Some landing,' Ivory tried to make a joke of it.

Eyes deeper than coal stared back at her.

'You find humour in my fall?' The voice older than Jacob bordered on a whisper.

'What happened to you?'

'What happened to *you?*'

Ginny's gaze moved past Ivory and took note of the hut in the distance.

Without word, she began moving towards it. But boys will be boys, and these ones were red hot with curiosity. They circled the seer like vultures and pecked at her with questions. She pushed past and they came again with renewed bother. Ginny halted them with a look.

And because Ginny was unreachable to them, her eyes resembling war, the twins imprinted, like baby ducklings, on Ivory.

The hut stood further than it seemed. Land rolled towards them, behind them. When Ivory's feet grew stones, the boys tugged her between them. But soon as her feet recovered, they lost goodwill, forgot Ivory, and braved Ginny once more with a new spurt of questions:

'What yous name?'

She turned.

'What *yous* name?' she said.

The first twin's jaw dropped, his astonishment at the fluency of Ginny's tongue. His recovery was instant. 'What yous first?'

She stopped.

'I seer,' she said. She gave them her 'don't argue' look. 'Yous game me and see what happen.'

Ku, Doh, the names tumbled out.

'Good,' said Ginny. 'I'm glad that be said. That there be Ivory. Ask why she name Ivory.'

And, all the way to the hut, the boys committed to the task.

7.

Ku and Doh yap yapped all the way, badgering Ivory. She minded it, and she didn't. There was no space before her, behind her – it was a marvel she could walk. The boys crowded her when they weren't rolling and tumbling so full of life, so sunny and unlike the sullen children of the foster homes. These ones pulled her and pinched her in a friendly way, spilled upon her their mischief and it filled her with humour. They pestered her like siblings, family she never knew, like a good foster family.

8.

She looked at the twins and, though she was all grown up, she imagined herself as a little girl again, and the boys the children you would find in a good foster home. Before long, she was laughing and chasing after them, nearly rolling and tumbling herself, how full of life.

Together, beneath a reddening sky, the four of them crossed another field, olive and peppered with gladioli and orange banksias. Finally, beyond the rainbow meadow, Ginny at the fore, they arrived at a dirt road. A path led to a ramshackle fence well worn with ants, if not age. The posts gaped free, gateless.

Inside the compound, a merry flame outside a mud hut bubbled broth in a blackened pot on three hearthstones. Other than a fearless scurry of lizards across the yard, no living thing stood in sight.

Coal eyes turned towards the twins.

'Where yous folk?'

'Mama Pebble –' twin said.

'She inside –' another said.

The boys burst into the hut and, with notable din, emerged with a woman leaning on a cane. Black wattle, Ivory observed, and it much resembled the digging stick that had once accompanied Ginny's walk through desert country. It seemed centuries, now, since Ivory had journeyed to Orange Crater, to fetch the medicine woman for Operation Limelight. From the look of things, it was dogged Ginny who had fetched Ivory.

Mama Pebble wore the ageless skin of a child, her face smooth as butter. Only the curl of her back, the ash in hair completely disarrayed, marked age. She stood lightly curved yet tall at the doorway of the hut. Her gaze was fogged. Her lips moved wordlessly.

'Mama Pebble, look!' Doh pointed at Ginny.

'Mama Pebble, look!' Ku tugged at Ivory's arms, displaying her as if she were a toy.

If there were something initial in Mama Pebble's reaction, her walk careful, her gaze was completely hollow. A breeze lifted the hem of her skirt, the colour of tree bark, above which was nothing but a flesh-coloured strip that covered her breasts. She bent to the ground, to a woven rug bearing dried grubs. She stirred them, turned them with her fingers. She smiled. 'Ahm,' she said.

'We sick,' one twin said.

'Mama Pebble sick,' another said.

They looked at Ginny, and then Ivory. 'Yous sick?' they said in unison.

Suddenly it clicked. Ivory remembered the purple-haired twins of Bahati's tale. The loin-clothed boys who unleashed a *buntu* from the rib of a calabash. That explained the bizarreness of this world: Ginny Mo'unga had torpedoed them into the Valley of Dreams: land that had pulsed with indignation that fed to outrage and cataclysmic climatic change when an evil deed was done and fire burnt, keen as lust, to cook a man whole; land that had climbed to the galaxies in search of a nobler world.

But that story was not a current affair; it was eons ago. A myth! So how could the boys be here? And why were they still boys?

9.

Ginny made herself comfortable. She entered the hut and emerged with something in a gourd that she drank.

Ivory erred on the side of caution. She sat on the ground, leaned her back against the seamless outside wall of the hut. She looked at one boy. 'Ku!' He came running. She smiled, finally she had got it. For all their likeness, she could tell them apart.

'So why yous fly in sky?'

'Ask the medicine woman.'

'Yous seer?'

He pestered her with questions but Ivory asked one of her own: 'How did Mama Pebble go mad?'

'Muntu rise from calabash tip.'

'Mushroom man, he make and break itself like ash,' cried Doh.

'Yes, he dirt and ash!' cried Ku.

'He roar!' they chimed.

Ginny, burping whatever it was she had drunk from the gourd, set about fixing the hut. Pots and wooden spoons clamoured inside.

'... touch beast dust.'

'... she gone mad.'

Words floated above Ivory.

'... bring curse.'

'... we sick.'

'... we all sick.'

'... I hungry.'

Ginny came out of the hut.

'Ku. Doh.' Her fingers clicked. 'Bring spear-thrower.'

'Why yous want spear-thrower?'

'I fix Mama Pebble.'

'How yous fix her?'

'Bring the spear-thrower.'

10.

Ivory was not counting time, but it was a good walk and her heels were beginning to ache. Along the way, Ginny found a strong stick whose tip she shaped with a rock into a spear. They arrived at the lip of the forest in broad daylight, but each step inside the woodland was like walking into a dusk filled with silence.

How black it was by the time they reached a clearing in the belly of the forest. The world here had a life of its own. A murky air trailed them, pulsed as if it were living – Ivory could hear the heartbeat – and it shadowed them, circled them until they were imprisoned inside its fog.

One tree stood tall in the clearing and Ginny was focused on that. It was a giant mandisa pine tree, tiered with branches, pregnant with leaves. High up in the night were rain clouds like a dark brow in the sky.

The footpath fell down the forest towards the silence of distilled wind. Ivory waited for the wind to respond but only got the topaz eyes of a white wolf in the dusk. She shook her head and the wolf disappeared. But she believed what she was now seeing were wrinkles in the big slant of tree ahead, and expected to see a sign that said, 'Mostly fools this way.' Her thirst was an ache and she wondered if in this surreal world she might see a vending machine with a concierge who took touch: 'How much for a drink?' One touch. But there was no vending machine and certainly no concierge. Just Ginny, Ivory and the boys approaching a mandisa pine tree.

The medicine woman led the way straight to the middle of the forest. Ivory trod through bush grass soft as emu hair, the boys nearly clinging to her legs, bumping into her from behind. They walked into a perimeter of cold air, and the medicine woman halted them with a hand that held the spear-thrower.

Up close the tree was not aslant, but rather stood with her malevolence. She waved her giant arms and fat fingers of green. With a low rumble, she shot a quiver of twigs like arrows, and the boys squealed and scattered. Ivory's thirst vanished. A tremor like an earthquake shook the ground, and it began to break with cracks.

The medicine woman rolled her eyes, only whites now, and began a chant around the tree. It sounded like: 'Oom-ba! Oom-ba!' Ivory followed Ginny and picked up the chant. The cheeta boy twins followed Ivory and picked up the chant. 'Oom-ba! Oom-ba!'

The air around the tree warmed. The ground went still, no more cracks formed. No more arrows of twigs shot at them and before long there was a sound of snoring. The tree had gone to sleep.

Ginny attached the handcrafted spear into the thrower. Still chanting, eyes rolled backward, she found the spear's balance point, tipped it and took aim. She ran forward then threw. The spear sang upwards... and then silence.

Ivory and the twins looked at each other.

Suddenly, a branch high up shook, and *crash!* A mandisa cone the size of a grown man's head rolled on the ground.

They walked out of the black forest, straight into daylight. The twins took turns carrying the mandisa cone. They huffed and puffed but would not accept help carrying it.

Back at Mama Pebble's hut, Ginny chanted as she slit open the mandisa cone with a knife rock from Mama Pebble's arsenal. Inside the cone were nearly a hundred nuts. The medicine woman dug a small hole in which she buried a few nuts. She covered the hole with clay soil, and lit a fire above it.

'Bring Mama Pebble.'

The boys led their mother and sat her near the fire.

'Bring cabbage palm.'

The boys sourced some branches that Ginny threw onto the fire. The green caught fire and released a pungent odour. As she had done in the forest, the medicine woman led an *Oom-ba!* chant around the smoke.

Ivory and the boys took up the chant around Mama Pebble, who sat on her haunches, oblivious to the smoke, picking and eating honey ants off the ground.

'Spirit a Great Chief Goanna!' cried Ginny.

'Ururu!' chanted the boys.

'Spirit a land!'

'Ururu!'

'Spirit a rock!'

'Ururu!'

'Spirit a mountain!'

'Ururu!'

Ivory's amulet glowed with the song, heated her skin.

They sang of a rainbow serpent whose weave curled a brow on the land, a brow that melted and planted its coil deeper into the ground to form a river. A river whose spirit danced and laughed with the people.

'Ururu!'

They told the story of seasons and colour and hope and pain and sadness. Of a man, a shape, a tree of ash, a thing that was also a buntu.

'Ururu!'

Of the loveliness of Dotto, and how that beauty was trapped in the valley of gloom...

'Ururu!'

They told of light and darkness and grey that eternally hid from coloured sky, rich like a painting, in a place where day and night were the same. They told of a woman whose mind had slipped, whose wisdom and kindness her sons still needed, whose healing would begin the calming of a curse...

'Ururu!'

At the end of the purging ceremony, the seer chewed a leaf. With an apostrophe of spit, she made a paste and rubbed it on Mama Pebble's fogged eyes. And the blindness eased off the woman's mind.

11.

'It will take time,' said the seer.

It did. Mama Pebble's recovery came in fits and starts.

Sometimes she sat still as a dead coolabah tree, colourless eyes unfocussed in space. The next moment she was walkabout, the curse in her eyes gone. In such times, when she was not telling stories in a voice that was poignant as a poem, she was brass as Picasso, loud as his colours.

She remembered nothing of the sickness that took her mind the moment she touched Doh's arm. She remembered everything else but didn't seem to notice the presence of her visitors. She walked past them, looked through them, didn't turn when Ginny or Ivory spoke.

The twins didn't understand their mother's lack of awareness, but they didn't question it.

Her museum voice thundered in echoes but the twins engaged her like a playmate.

'We sick no more,' they cried, merry little larrikins bold as gold.

They couldn't get enough of the buttery nuts from the mandisa cone once Ginny dug them up from the clay. When they weren't stuffing their faces with food, or buried to their necks in mischief, the boys fought.

Ivory had learnt to fight when she was a child, swung a fist from when she was just little at St Vincent's, and had by now mastered the art. But she was amazed to see Ku and Doh fighting, because it was pointless – they had no reason to, no one was taking or snatching anything, so there was no reason for defence, theirs was just a natural progression from play.

Ku was the master fist, he reminded Ivory of her fighting days when she knocked everything down. Doh was the champion foot, he reminded Ivory of her childhood, how she sometimes threw a leg over the fence, hauled after her the garbage bag that held her possessions – including the tiny photo frame and tattered Janey – before she hit the ground running, only to be found and brought back to punishment.

12.

Sitting with the seer and watching the boys, Ivory found voice to ask what she'd long been avoiding.

'Tell me about my father.'

Ginny studied her a long time.

'He was just a boy. He came from a family of eleven, a middle child. But the smoke chose him to become the elder of the native people, and the amulet agreed.'

'Was he special?' asked Ivory.

'He wasn't much, but he was a sporty fella and loved the footy. He wasn't big, others could easily knock him over. But he was a natural forward with pace in his legs. He could kick a twig, a pebble or a ball and bend it to go where he wanted.'

'Fancy that – he knew how to put a ball between the posts,' said Ivory. 'I guess that made him some kind of special.'

'He gathered urchins and bushed them out with footy clinics. He taught them to arch low and skid with the instinct of a hare in a dodge, to leap like a kangaroo and get a good mark for possession of the ball, to put the body right with the weight of a koala and smother the other team with a tackle to the ground. He taught them to swoop with the accuracy of an eagle and spot where members of their teams were scattered for a good pass, to snatch a ball with the agility of a dingo, bounce it, bounce it as they ran, and in full pace kick it outside 50 meters through the posts. He was always barking instructions and the little ones listened.'

Ivory smiled. 'I can picture that.'

'Some tourist scout spotted him and that's what got him to Melbourne. But he wasn't cut out for the big smoke. Melbourne and its temperament of an aunt who gives you roasted lizard and squeezes you to her bosom moments before she wallops the daylights out of you. Just when you think you're right, the weather slams you. Melbourne with its fashion, graffiti, trams, theatres and flea markets. Melbourne with its gentleman clubs, and girls who stand with the night down alleyways, who smoke cigarette after cigarette and go home with strangers to bed them. He abandoned the city and its promise of making him a star, and went back to teaching little ones in the wilderness country. One of the kids in his clinic went on to top five draft pick and joined a team in Western Sydney. Another was a championship player for some team in Melbourne or Brisbane. By now people understood that his calling as an elder of the native people was to motivate children.'

'So why did he hook up with my mother?'

'Why? That's a loaded question. Nobody knows why. When this runaway girl with big eyes, scruffy hair and a drug habit rocked up in the wilderness country, who knows? Maybe she reminded him of those girls with cigarettes in their mouths, nonchalant in the moonlit promiscuous streets of St Kilda in Melbourne, and he felt pity.'

13.

That was the first of their many conversations. One day, as Ivory lowered herself to sit on the ground beside Ginny, the medicine woman surprised her with new words.

'You're here to question.'

Ivory regarded her. 'Back at the Tiffany Hotel, you promised me a journey.'

'Isn't being here a journey?'

'A journey has purpose and I feel that mine hasn't started.' The amulet was like a burning rock on her skin. 'I have a prophetic stone to return.'

Ginny laughed out loud and clapped her hands. 'I knew you were special.' She looked at Ivory. 'It's not the dog in the fight, it's the fight in the dog. You've got the mongrel.' She was silent a moment. 'But are you ready?'

'The amulet seeks its rightful owner, whether or not I am ready.'

The medicine woman watched her closely, a strange expression on her face.

'You are resilient. I saw it the day you sought me in the wilderness country. I saw it in desert country as you hobbled without wince from Orange Crater to Dick-a-Dick, when blisters

covered your heels and every nerve in your body sang. I saw it.
And now here you are, that hardship forgotten. A truth awaits
you.'

'Teach me.'

'It's right here.' Ginny's crooked finger touched Ivory's
breast. 'You don't need teaching. You have the ability to ease the
suffering in Muntu's soul.'

'How?'

'Bring him to the place of dreams. He must find peace.'

'How?'

'How, indeed.'

Ivory sighed. 'What if I'm afraid?'

'You don't have to wait for the fear to go. The fear never fully
goes. But remember what I said, sometimes it takes a terrible fear
to bring out your greatest strength.'

And then Ivory remembered and encountered a real fear.
'Bahati!'

'What about him?'

'If it's a sex jini –' she coloured, remembered the tantra just
before the buntu. 'Is he dead?'

'No.'

'Will he die?' her voice small.

'You can save him, guide the buntu out safely.'

'Why hasn't the buntu –' she swallowed. 'Why hasn't it killed
Bahati yet?'

'The energy of fulfilment nourishes it. And then it uses that
same energy to force out from its prey, killing them.'

'But Bahati –'

'He withheld his energy. That is why the buntu is still trapped
inside.'

'Without Bahati –' her voice broke.

'You must find Muntu. Bahati cannot carry a buntu within
him for the rest of his life. Slowly it will kill him.'

'How do we release it?'

'Find Muntu. Only he can call to his twin soul.'

'What about the women? Those like Mama Pebble; the women whose minds the buntu tarnished?'

'The purging ceremony that healed Mama Pebble – it spread healing to all victims of the curse. And they do not remember, just as Mama Pebble doesn't. They know not of the sickness that took them, how it happened. Or why.'

Nine: Finding the Seer

1.

All Ivory knew was to walk. She trod on until the swell in her ankles spread to her toes.

'Walk?' she had said to Ginny, aghast. 'To where shall I walk?'

The medicine woman swirled her drink. 'To the blink of the stars,' she said without glancing up.

Ivory laughed.

'Look overhead,' Ginny pointed. 'The arrangement of the stars is linear. But the line thickens west. Head westward until you come to the largest cluster that blinks loudest. That's the end of the world.'

'And then what?'

'Listen to the amulet. It has inner fire and intuition. It will beacon its rightful owner.'

And so it began.

It was Ginny, not Mama Pebble, who warmed water for a bath. Ivory took it behind Grevillea shrubbery, scooped with a

Coolamon dish, scrubbed with a coil of Mitchell grass. She emerged, wrapped, the borrowed bark cut to the size of Mama Pebble who was a rather tall woman. Everything was in place for the voyage.

The boys, normally flying high, playful like kittens, today stood potbellied, immovable in her path like twin pillars.

'She go alone,' said Ginny.

Doh opened his mouth to protest but caught the set of Ginny's lips.

A fern necklace slung a pouch that held a twig toothbrush, a wrapped leaf of possum oil to keep at bay crawlies and flying insects. A hair-string belt clasped a water gourd and twists of dough, crisped over a clay skillet in the belly of a hearth stone fire.

'You have only to look,' said Ginny, her touch solid on Ivory's shoulder.

A flood of energy wove through Ivory, and her vision swam. A cloud in her head obscured thought. In an instant tranquillity spread, a float of wisdom that engulfed her.

Suddenly Ivory knew what she must do.

'The gift of your ancestors,' medicine woman said.

And Ivory walked.

2.

She strode out west from the bold colours of Mama Pebble's world until the grassland, taller than it had seemed from a distance, fell behind. Fatigue crept into legs. So when she saw a saltbush, she bled its sap to ease her pain.

She sat briefly under the umbrella of a thick fern. Rested somewhat, she faced the stars and continued her walk. She walked until she came to a cluster of stars that blinked loud and sure at the mouth of a forest, woods that cracked with lightning.

Left to the corridor of trees stood a mighty crag. Ivory camped. She sank gratefully beneath the monstrous eave of the rock, wrapped arms about herself and faced the forest where another spit of lightning chased a bellow of thunder.

Bahati… He was her river, her mountain, her rock.

The man she loved was in peril. The man who had seen at once the ivory inside an abused Izett, a tired, tired girl with ice-green eyes who had lost her childhood and everything called home from the moment she was born. She had lost it over and over with such freshness of the loss when a man from a basement club gave her a look. It was a look that brought out the little girl who fought everyone and everything to mask the loneliness of her tiny world, only then she was sixteen and a day. Bahati, he was her beautiful man inside out. Would she see him again?

Glum, she hugged her thoughts.

Rain fell.

Ivory huddled against the black rock, monstrous as a devil's marble. A gush of falls from the crag's edge swept into the forest until, overwhelmed, her eyes hollowed and a steal of sleep crept over her. A breeze in the opposite direction sprayed globules of water to touch her face.

Suddenly, she was afraid.

3.

Her solitude was a tattoo in her chest, but you cannot tattoo a disquieted inner child and nobody wanted to get caught holding the door of a moving house that got slippery when filled with the tears of an itinerant little girl. She was crying because one half of her was walking with a pocket full of salt across the threshold of the moving house in a wasteland full of dead trees. It did not matter if the house was in the wasteland or the wasteland was in the house; all that mattered was that her other half was sitting in a prepaid-fare taxi with a flaming crown that was racing to nowhere but everywhere in a night that was dark as witching soot. On her lap she held the familiar scent of her mother's ghost inside a garbage bag full of intimate belongings, and that is how it stayed.

Suddenly she woke. She rubbed her eyes.

She remembered the moments before her sleep, gazing ahead at velvet darkness in the forest. Inside her loneliness, she had nestled against the rock and hugged her knees. She hadn't waited long for sleep. It claimed her.

Now she was fully awake. The crag towered above and arched into a natural eave of stone that shielded like an umbrella from a cascade of rain.

She trembled slightly, not from cold.

A sense of strangeness enveloped her, adding weight to the task ahead which included going beyond that forest. Sounds were coming from it. Whispers. Or was it a rustle of wind? She tried to shrug off apprehension. Beyond the leaves, the twigs, the fog, within the belly of that forest, something was *not* waiting for her. *Nothing* was waiting for her. She thought the words over and over. Nothing was waiting for her.

Gradually rain became a swish. Silvered drips scattered sideways not straight, distanced from the gush of before. Ivory watched the drizzle stretch away into the greedy forest that swallowed it whole inside a fluster of shrubbery. She sat sad and alone and irritable and hungry and bloated all at once. Those little dough balls… She uncapped her gourd and swigged from it. The water was tepid. She tucked the gourd between her feet and waited. *Drip! Drip!* droplets from the arched zenith. She was alone.

Her solitude was a fear, not just an actuality. She missed Ginny and her crooked finger and her scent like bush mint.

A throb of thunder shook the grey forest. Rain in fits and starts, she thought. Was that how it was? How it would be? Sitting there hugging herself, pioneer and forbear of Operation

Limelight brought to galaxy wilderness by a clairvoyant woman, she thought about… things. Like a shop in Sydney that had once drawn her. It was a quiet little place, all seedy, with one stained window marked *Repair*.

It was a day after she put fresh flowers on Sister Immaculata's grave at Kemps Creek. The site held a stone cross, its limestone flaking, and plastic flowers at the foot in disrepair despite the kind of fake sheen one might get at a funeral home in Las Vegas. It saddened her to witness the decay, the thrift in the fittings Sister Hildegarde (the cunning crow) had authorised. Such mismatched reality. Of all the nuns, Sister Immaculata was the most valuable to the young lives she briefly touched on their way in and out of St Vincent's. All this time since the nun's passing, Ivory didn't know how to say goodbye.

Something stirred – a leaf, a voice in the wind, the rustle of a tunic, a sigh rising from her feet. She looked, nothing there.

'You're a hero. A real fire cracker,' said Sister Immaculata from the grave. 'Hero… hero… fire cracker.' The words looped from the grave, over and over.

She remembered how Sister Immaculata had often called on her during chores into the night. Not only to hearten her but to pass on the calming in her presence, in the lilt of her voice. The young Izett was grateful of the nun's kindness, but was sometimes uninclined to whisper anything nice or funny back, as she hand-washed the library floors in their marbled serenity. But Sister Immaculata didn't mind. She would take to her knees and scrub alongside. Even at midnight, there was a sweet aroma of baking, warm honey and cinnamon, wafting from the kitchen below. Or was it the scent of Sister Immaculata with her white tunic and a nurse's cape?

Ivory's own mother had somehow lost her. Ivory never thought of her much, not any more. But she longed for Sister Immaculata with such agony, nothing compared.

Back in the city from Kemps Creek, coffee in hand, the Styrofoam cup warm still, no carry carton, Ivory was contemplating the ruin she had left behind at Kemps Creek when she found herself standing at the corner of Spring and Jutten Roads, gazing at the littered lane she hadn't noticed before. But there it was – Route Lane, the poster said. Urine maps and matching smells layered a derelict surface secret with knowledge, a full DNA bank.

Delicately, Ivory weaved her way towards the seedy shop with its stained window marked *Repair*. Inside was a young woman with a sultry Olivia look – which Olivia, Ivory didn't know, but that was her first instinct when she saw the woman, bohemian frock and all. Sultry Olivia.

'Yes?' Sultry's airless voice, her liquid lava eyes penetrating.

'What do you repair?'

'What do you want repaired?'

'A watch?'

'You left it on your dresser, and it's good as gold.'

'What?'

'And the name's wrong,' Sultry said.

'I beg your pardon?'.

'Said the name's wrong. And your watch is fine.'

Ivory touched her empty wrist inside a long sleeve.

The woman edged over the counter.

'So what is it really that you so badly want repaired?'

Ivory smiled, excused herself and left without another word.

'Soon,' the woman had said behind her back.

It wasn't a threat, Ivory somehow knew. Not from some mind-reading bitch, it wasn't.

'Soon.'

It was a promise.

4.

Rain had just ended.

A twinkle of light swept through the fog inside the forest wall. Ivory puzzled about the light. She moved to rise but her foot had gone to sleep. She couldn't feel her estranged toes. When she tried again, nothing moved, just her thoughts in bits and bobs. Muntu. Ancestor! Find him. Where? Everything was altogether strange and remote. Sydney. If she sought it again, would she find Route Lane? And Sultry Olivia? Could other people see the lane, find the shop, understand something of what Olivia might tell them? It was clearly important because Ivory didn't so badly need repair now. And she was here. She was beginning to understand more about herself, and to accept that perhaps she was special.

Suddenly she felt her toes, her entire foot. She flexed her knees and stretched them. Aiding her rise with a hand against the rock, she walked to the eave where water still dripped and pattered. She put out a tongue and tasted a chilled drop.

Up in the sky, the stars were gone. So was the deep redness that marked the skyline. Now white clouds danced in a sea of blue. Night or day? A fresh wind touched her cheek. And then there were hawks, circling overhead around the sleeve of the woodland where a grim fog had lurked. The fog was gone, paled by the new steal of light. Ivory could now see trees, branches like amputated arms. Below, kinky grass swayed. Something rattled inside, wispy sighs waiting for her. She remembered the sentient mandisa pine. But she also remembered the medicine woman's words: 'You don't have to wait for the fear to go'.

She walked away from the crag and stood at the fringe of the forest. She faced a cluster of snow trees with droopy branches that hung like a wizard beards. A breeze brushed her hair. Resolute, she plunged through the corridor of branches into the brush of a startled bat. She staggered, surprised by a burst of new colour, a yawn of land so bright it was a kaleidoscope.

The forest was an illusion.

5.

The glen was swathed in song: Birdsong. Toad song. Wind song. Water song.

An ocean of grass carried a magnificent hue of jade that vacillated in colour to sapphire. A slow running creek quavered with crystal white water. More water, sea green, spurted out of a rise on the ground along the creek and slithered its way down the rock. By the time it fed into the deep belly of the river, it was purified, crystal white as the rest.

Ivory knelt and cupped crisp water, raised it to eager lips and drank. It was sweet at the tip of her tongue, a taste of fruit – banana or pear – as she swallowed. A gentle tang touched and lifted from the base.

Naked plains strode far out, beyond grass so virginal it stroked like velvet. Ivory followed the grass until it dipped to a valley alight with sound: a tinkle of china; soft bells in the wind; a scatter of beads on a surface; a soft pop or a whistle; the coo of a child; the purr of a slow approaching car... Sometimes there was music, so alien, so divine, it was alluring as a jewel.

She remembered walking with Bahati in the city one mid-morning on a weekend and he was telling her about his favourite native plant. 'It's black and droopy like Iceland poppies and has a halo of chandelier noir leaves.'

They came to an alley that cut through the second and third streets. It crawled with coffee shops littered with tourists. A parting stood in the middle of tables for two, four or six and a spontaneous crowd was beginning to gather around a sweet melody. She pushed through the throng and found the young violin player with his tight curls and tight jeans and flowing passion. Music rose and wobbled as he shifted the violin, as he moved his hand and fingers and tapped a foot on the rhythm machine aground. Her eyes gobbled his immersion, his whole body attuned to the music. He was young, maybe nineteen, and she could only think of liberty. She found something freeing in the music and swayed to its autumn, the unrecognisable yet familiar melody that made people stop and respond. A few feet away, an open violin case spilled five and ten-dollar notes, some gold coins, and a furry toy: a tiny bird with a white cushion body and shiny pearl eyes, blue rimmed. She ripped a note from her wallet and placed it on the little bird's beak. In a daze, she snatched Bahati's hand and tore herself and him from the bird with its hypnotic gaze and the boy with his curly mop and the music flowing from his belly with its shadow of seasons and folklore and something close to druids.

This music of the plains was just as alluring, and the sound w grew richer with her approach. Now it sounded more birdlike – a choir of swans or pelicans or kookaburras or swallows. Bars varied with wind. The vale loped and dropped, carpeted by golden plants, bushy plants, lavender plants, snowy plants. Then it rose, climbed to a tumble of hills crowned with burgundy trees that turned out to be bamboo. By this time, Ivory, pushed for breath, was convinced it was the sound of singing birds. But she could see no sign of them.

She followed the song uphill. Halfway, she saw the birds. At first they were silver dots in the sky, opening and closing like petals. Then they flew closer to the ground, a float of sweet melody, loud and rich and spreading. They sang, flawless in their pattern of flight, wings opening and closing in unison, equidistant to each other.

As they winged away, something pushed over the bamboo hill in a sudden gust that brought a stab of fear. A marsh rot from luminous green bog thick as jelly stood between the rising land and the bamboo trees ahead. She was in the process of circling the bog when her foot broke through the land, earth that dampened and softened, and it swallowed her heel. The more she struggled, the deeper she sank. Her other foot was also sinking. Now she was ankle-deep in murk. The bog was alive, and it was growing around her, surrounding her. A life form that gripped, sucked, swallowed her deeper. Now she was knee-deep, half-cursing, half-sobbing, clawing at grass that collapsed.

She clasped something thin but solid, a bony plant. Gasping, she shimmied, bellied, out of the bobbing mud. She climbed with her hands and drew herself to her feet until she was head level with a being and almost threw up her heart.

6.

Waist up, the thing was never still. Feet growing from ground, its neck constantly moved. The being swayed from side to side, eyes aglow. It looked at her sidelong from a swinging head filmed with a screen of gelatinous scales. Its body was the same shade of green as the bog that had swallowed her.

'W-what are you!' at last she stammered.

The being did not answer, and did not appear bewildered by Ivory's presence.

She wondered if it spoke English.

Its eyes rolled and snapped and veered west and then east. Its pupils vanished into the corner and came back. Ivory noticed the two of them were not alone. An army was rising out of the luminous ground, spilling across green jelly that now covered the prairie.

She hoped this was the zenith of delusion, but none of them vanished with a blink. A train of naked beasts with rolling eyes bore down on her. Bewildered, she turned her gaze toward the single entity regarding her. It seemed to be the leader, the way the others bowed to it.

'Do you speak English?' almost a whisper.

The thing blinked.

Ivory blinked.

'I fright to you.'

'You speak!' she cried. 'English!'

'Tell to me,' it astounded her further with its reedy voice. 'I fright to you?' It waited for a response.

She had no provision for an intelligent gelatine being.

'Yes,' she said slowly. 'You frighten me.'

'Face to me,' it said.

She lifted her eyes until they embraced those frightful ones.

'Thank to me,' it said.

'Thank you!'

'No. Thank to me.'

'Thank to –' It was thanking her, she realised, for the courtesy of holding its gaze.

'Ask to me,' it said.

'I don't understand.'

'Why you do here!'

So, hoping it would understand and believe, Ivory told of her mission. She spoke of Earth and of the buntu on a killing spree. She spoke of Ginny, a seer who had lifted her to the Valley of Dreams. She spoke of Muntu, trapped in the sea of nothingness.

'If I can find him, perhaps I can re-unite him with his twin and the buntu will find the place of dreams.'

'Tell to me big task.'

To Ivory, one thing was clear: it understood. It did not dispute her borderless mission beyond portals of Earth. And now that she relaxed, she saw something more in the creature: its face told of nobility.

'Gaze to me –'

She looked where it pointed towards the forest of bamboo.

'Palace to me.'

'But how?' Ivory stammered. 'How did you know I was thinking of nobility?' And then it dawned. 'You are telepathic. You can read my thoughts.'

It moved its face in what was possibly a smile.

'I Goth,' it said. 'Not it. Please. Tell to me. Goth.'

'Goth,' she said. 'Can you read *all* my thoughts?'

7.

The forest of bamboo was another illusion. As soon as Ivory pushed past a cluster of stems, she walked through the gates of a new world gripped in twilight.

Goth spread his arms. 'Carthasis welcome to you.'

Fat stars and a half-moon gleamed light across cobbled ground. She caught glimpses in the distance of a towered building that was, Ivory felt sure, the fragment of a civilized world.

The column of gelatinous soldiers behind her moved quietly, fluidly. Goth spilled along.

The air carried a lively aroma of tea or pleasant smoke, something warm and balanced. Before reaching the tower, a womanoid with a baby and a chase of three children spilled towards and poured into Goth's outstretched arms.

'Woman to me,' her host introduced them.

The womanoid nodded her way.

'Your wife?'

'Mælda.' He lingered on the strange mid-vowel. 'She name Mælda.'

The children were bashful, not pretty. 'Little River, Crimson Vale. And this – Lu'cient.'

Ivory regarded the infant, appealing in its playfulness, loathsome in its gelatinous fluidity.

'He name V'arnis. Crown Prince.'

Ivory glanced at the heir, whose malevolent eyes watched her with dislike of astonishing magnitude. Taken aback, she turned her gaze to Goth.

'You are a king then?'

'King Goth of Carthasis. Come to mine. Mælda cook to us fine dinner.'

Indeed, Mælda had feathers and blood in her pouring skin. She had just killed a bird, Goth explained, for Mælda spoke no word. Nobody else, it appeared, spoke.

Ivory followed him into a star-shaped courtyard bursting with activity, where subjects – delighted as they were at their king's return from something momentous – exhibited no effort to hide interest in the newcomer. Gelatine children with bald heads, swaying necks and half-wild eyes that throbbed like energy fields, trailed the king and his entourage through a private entrance into a garden. Flowers exuded a nose of citrus. And tea.

Bathed, watered, Ivory luxuriated in the status of imperial guest. But it was a basking in a horror story. Goth boasted of his kingdom, flew her around the city, wall to wall, in what he called a Xen-flyer. It was a shuttle that veered dangerously through thin space and swept high above the cones of hills until her head swam. With gestures of hand, he impressed upon her towering fortresses and imposing machinery whose glitter sang.

A building drew close. It was a revolving castle with crystal wings and spiked protrusions upon which bodies were impaled. Bodies distorted with rods, arms and legs still moving.

'Traitors to me,' Goth dismissed the gruesome sight. His eyes took a hue that was difficult to catch.

Ivory grew small into the hatch that held her intact inside the aircraft. Her fear was of a kind she had never experienced before. The shuttle eddied and wove through ten slanting pillars, before soaring high above an antennaed steeple of a temple-shaped structure.

'Secondary palace.'

The Xen-flyer climbed down. At the foot of a ridged cobalt hillock, Goth indicated with his chin – or whatever took its place – a station where other magnificent flyers rested. He pointed at shadowed ruins that signified an epoch, he said, a time in history. Now, battalions of builders worked by day to restore its full opulence.

'Seat of government to be.'

Ivory made out a brazen head in the shape of Goth.

It was near dusk when they returned. Goth's palace of quartz, granite and bluestone was lit to blinding. It bleached the starlight.

Inside, servants greeted them with bowls of scorching porridge or broth alive with heat and flavour that mellowed, not bewildered, Ivory's head. The potage weaved sweetly down her throat and settled lightly in her stomach. Inside a wash of relaxation, or perhaps it was something in the broth, she no more minded about bodies impaled on spikes atop a fortress.

8.

Goth considered her sidelong. they sat on refined marble that sparkled, set on a pergola that faced a sootless fire whose tongues emitted flames so bright, they turned crimson, then burnt orange, then blue, and back to crimson.

Ivory gazed at the choreography of flames, loops moulding loops, patterns weaving patterns; at Mælda serving platters and platters of meats and sweetbreads; at delicacies that filled Ivory's mouth with refined tastes of something natural and deep: berry, honey, cinnamon, vanilla, truffle, oak, fennel, earth, pepper, melon, peach and a new fragrance of foods she had never encountered. Heady scents wafted in the air and lit her to euphoria… Ice-cold drinks carried flavour that pushed boundaries, whiffs that were a blend of vibrant, intense, acid, sublime, tropical, complex, balanced, soft, creamy, grained, buttery…

Fed to bursting, calmed by sustenance and the lightness of Goth's manner, Ivory's wariness slipped. She could live here forever, she thought giddily. Ginny could find a way to bring Bahati. And Slobber. Life would be wild and simple. She struggled to retain sensibility, and lost. In its place now crept a vagrant mood of conflict and nostalgia she could not quite grip. There was something light about the air. The choreography of flames looped, patterned. The nostalgia. She found herself speaking of Earth and of Bahati: the kindliness of his face and the exact tilt and shade of it, the tan of his arms and the tar black richness of the curls that also wove an island on his chest.

She speaks of Earth and of Bahati: the kindliness of his face and the exact tilt and shade of it…

'Tell to me,' Goth encourages, 'of parent.'

So she speaks of the parents she never knew, of an orphaned road desolate from a mother's love, abandoned from a father's protection.

'…no grave or headstone. I never ran my fingers along the letters of his name, imagined the sort of man he might have been.'

Of foster carers she speaks little, for that path evokes hurtful memories.

Of foster carers she had little to say, that path evoked hurtful memories.

Goth nodded.

Surrounding them, several beats away, sat Mælda, not quite pretty but not quite repulsive as before, now that Ivory was at ease and accommodating. Lu'cient sat on her mother's lap, eyes beginning to glide. She sucked at a thumb. A dozen womanoids and their brood, countless children of random sizes and ages – judging by the shape of blob – spilled over the gazebo. Everything was unusual; it carried an almost magical feel. Everybody was relaxed, except V'arnis, watchful as a sentry. The dislike in his baby eyes never wavered from Ivory's face. She imagined a placard on his forehead, a warning that said: *CAUTION – smiles when ravenous for flesh.*

She imagines a placard on the baby's forehead, a warning that says: CAUTION – smiles when ravenous for flesh.

'Harem to me.' Goth is pointing at the womanoids. 'V'arnis, he child, no fright to you.'

He laughs. The sound of his merriment, his laughter, is like the trickle of a stream that feeds into a river that swells and splashes into rocks. She laughs with him. And then, more solemn, she says, 'You must try not to read my mind. It is not polite.'

'I try to mask. You think too loud.'

His voice is of distinction, a big voice that rustles. He gazes at the dancing flames a moment, and his face becomes tighter, harsher, chiselled – if that is possible. Hewn as if from rock.

He gazed at the dancing flames a moment, and his face became tighter, harsher, chiselled – if that were possible. Hewn as if from rock.

Ivory absorbed it and pondered it and, in an unguarded moment, bent and lifted a carve of sweetbread to her mouth. It was fine-grained, biscuity, a gastronomic burst at the edge of her tongue. She turned towards her host with half a smile, and caught it back. For Goth's bulbous gelatinous head, its brain matter visible through clear skin, was a few skins from her face and, though he was smiling, his eyes had changed.

9.

The biscuit on Ivory's tongue became ash.

'Earth people no good to me. We war.'

Her trust came apart and drifted away, away, scattered.

'You fright – with reason,' Goth said. 'See that V'arnis? He child but he – formidable opponent.' Using the words of her thoughts. 'He tear apart weak sentient like you, claw like a rain of knives. Run like a shooting star.' His voice faded in and out. It crept and closed and crawled and morphed. 'His mind embroil. It bad intention to you. But I, Goth, I cloud to his intent. V'arnis fear displeasure to me. He good crown prince.' His gaze pierced.

His gaze is piercing.

Mælda and the womanoids seem closer. V'arnis is advancing on all fours.

'But I hospitality to you because mutual interest. Beast buntu, it kill here.' His voice disconnects from his body and appears from the night. 'You stop buntu, cheerful to me.'

In that instant, Ivory understands the buntu's lunar flights. Understands that not only did the demon terrorise Earth and a part of Mama Pebble's world; its attack spread to Carthasis and across galaxies. But she isn't taking any orders.

'Don't you or your gelatinous brood, br-ood, br...' She is beginning to slur. 'What-ever hap-pens...'

Sometimes it takes a terrible fear, fear, fear... chimes the medicine woman in her head.

To bring out your greatest strength, strength... chimed the medicine woman in her head.

If she could just get to her feet.... She felt profoundly weary. Her head was both heavy and weightless. Her heartbeat felt mild and delicate. Her eyelids were sluggish on blink, like slow motion. Faces, several, pressed down towards her. Blank faces, scored faces, swaying faces. The baby V'arnis was smiling. She tried to change the pattern of her blinks, but they grew wider apart.

As a terrible fear gripped her, she heard Sister Immaculata, the lilt in her voice soothing, as she looped her clear words. 'You're a hero. A real fire cracker.'

She hears Sister Immaculata, lilt in her clear words.

Ivory focuses and wills herself into a mind chant.

Spirit a Great Chief Goanna... Ururu.

The amulet warms against her skin. She looks, and the faces are fearful.

Spirit a Great Chief Goanna... Ururu... Spirit a land... Ururu...

The stone's heat against her skin grows twicefold. The faces are retreating.

Spirit a Great Chief Goanna... Ururu... Spirit a land... Ururu... Spirit a rock... Ururu... Spirit a mountain...Ururu!

The amulet is fully aglow, a bright orange that shimmers. The faces are gone.

The amulet fully glowed, it's auburn twinkling.

Ivory was filled with a discerning spirit. She pictured a meadow. Was it a destination or a space between? It didn't matter. She listened to a chime of bells, a sweet tinkling filled with a scent of flowers.

Spirit a Great Chief Goanna... Ururu... Spirit a land... Ururu... Spirit a rock... Ururu... Spirit a mountain...Ururu!

A door snapped open and threw her up into a gaping wound of planet.

A door snaps open with a sound like the crack of a bullet, and throws her up into a gaping wound of planet. Her scream is silent. Suddenly she is inside a maelstrom, swirl, swirl, floating on turbulence. Now she is swimming in waves, bobbing and weaving in a singularity of time. An aroma of wind touches her nostrils, wind with woodland flavour, so many layers of it. Wind.

She is suffocating.

10.

She lay sprawled, face up on a bed of wattle blossoms beneath a leafless dragon tree. It was like *déjà vu* and yet again not. She'd been here before, and she hadn't. A lone cloud on an emerald sky resembled an enlarged stroboscopic image of a dancer. She watched the polarised shadows and simulation. It was magnificent.

Her amulet shone like a shooting star.

She cradled a new thought, mused hazily on it. On this mission, nothing would improve. If she could just find her way back to the boys, to Mama Pebble's world, to Ginny...

A breeze stirred the grass.

Ivory cast away the temptation to abandon her mission to find Muntu, and guide him to his lost soul that was terrorising the worlds. She sat up. Her limbs felt much weakened.

She spied hillocks and vales north and could almost have sworn sight of dotted patterns in the horizon, the opening and closing of singing birds. But she remembered the green quagmire that almost sealed her in its belly, and she remembered Goth. How one minute he regarded her as if she amused him, then in a snap as if she was a meal. She climbed to her feet and headed in the direction of a trio of moons that smiled in the skyline.

The scene was meadow and jungle that stretched wide and far. Flowers sprawled and grew tall; flowers soft and fresh, they hadn't built a scent. A floating cloud appeared suddenly. It broke into a scatter of soundless birds resembling giant rosellas. They circled in a dance, swelled and filled the sky, until Ivory could clearly see short beaks sharpened to spearheads, and the edges of blue-tipped or well-blackened tails.

Sound erupted in screeches, metallic-like whistles. *Cooseek! Cooseek!* In a single wind, the birds came upon Ivory in a swoop. She cried out as they lifted her by her garments into the sky. She struggled, stopped thrashing when height became perilous. A knot clutched her belly and she felt nauseous. The beasts soared into a fuzzy world and, as one, released her.

Ivory dropped onto a soft grass bed that smelled of eucalyptus. She lay dazed. Up in the sky no sight or sound of the birds. Giddy, she rose unsteadily. She took a step forward, tottered and stumbled. Hemmed in by gloomed fog closing from all directions inside a howl of wind, she fell back onto the mound of eucalyptus.

11.

Disaster, it seemed to her, spawned from all directions. Ginny Mo'unga, medicine woman, had a lot of explaining to do.

'Who are you?'

Ivory jumped. The voice was tall, open and strong, a voice from a sea of nothingness. 'Who are you?' she asked in turn.

Slowly, fog lifted. She found herself the focus of eyes deeper than the sea. Nobody stood before her; just a set of black, black eyes.

'Why are you wearing my amulet?'

'Who are you?' she said again.

'Where did you get it?'

'My mother. Who are you?'

'I am Muntu. Who are you?'

Ginny's words came flooding back. 'It appears that I am your descendant,' she said in half a whisper.

'I see.' He did not question her identity. He accepted it. He stretched a hand and, as if he were a magnet, the amulet snapped from her neck and wound around his.

'It belongs here. Not you – why are you here?'

'We need to talk about your…twin soul.'

He went silent. Then: 'Do you know where he is?'

'No. Do you?'

'No.'

'Well he's causing mayhem.'

'What mayhem?'

'He seeks to find a path back to you. But he's killing people.'

'I see.'

'No, you don't. You have not sought re-union. All this time. Why?'

'My pursuit is of greater urgency.'

The voice was tranquil as drizzle, its gentleness completely lifting the remnants of grey air.

'Is it – Dotto?'

Wilderness swept into the eyes. 'What do you know –' the voice sagged – 'of Dotto?'

'Perhaps I can help you.' Ivory did not know why she said it. The words just came with a wisdom inside her.

Glint climbed into the wilderness eyes.

'Where –' a bubble in his voice, 'is she?'

Something moved. Suddenly he stood before her. He was a beautiful man, dark as night, naked as a nail. And, oh, how tall! Ivory sought evidence of his burning death when twinned souls came apart, but singed lashes and a whisper of smoke from his nose were all she could find.

'Where is Dotto?' he asked again.

'I know someone who can help you.'

His eyes closed. When he spoke, it was a voice inside a voice, torn from his throat, truthful as a harp. 'I've been waiting for you a long time.'

'I don't understand.'

'I knew from the start about twins.'

And though Ivory did not understand his words, she understood the rise and fall of his chest.

'Come with me,' she said.

12.

Their rapport was instant. His sincerity was staggering. He was the most genuine being, next to Bahati, that Ivory knew. His voice was like a steady column of quiet rain.

Hand in hand, they meandered through fields that sagged and lifted. Branches snapped at Ivory's face like claws, twigs shattered underfoot.

He was a man of shadows. Sorrow darkened his eyes and he only brightened when he spoke of Dotto, of reunion. Toying with reeds or grass in his hands, he would smile, his face aglow. But as soon as he stopped talking about his love, the ghost crept back into his eyes.

Despite the smallness of the forest and fog impairing her vision, Ivory saw a whole universe in it. How many kilometres they walked, she did not know. But they walked and walked, forever west, through land that climbed and fell, until Ivory was worn to a frazzle. They paused in the wilderness to feed on strong honey-sap bled from trees, and pushed on.

One day the fog lifted. They saw trees that stood long and sleek and fresh like virgins. Tall, climbing things that almost touched the big, green sky. Behind them, a necklace of red trees swayed around a yellow hill they had no recollection of climbing or descending.

Now wind roared furiously. Suddenly something struck Muntu to the ground. Much as he tried, he could take no further step ahead. An invisible wall knocked him down each attempt. 'Whatever stands beyond that wall, it is a world I cannot visit,' he said sadly. 'You must go alone.'

'I will come back, I promise.'

And just like that, he agreed. 'Tell her to close her eyes and think about the sea.'

13.

One step and Ivory's foot vanished into darkness. At once she was out of Muntu's world and into the middle of wet season. Whatever this was, wherever it was, it was shadowy.

Nervous the whole way, Ivory drew further inland and found herself in water-logged country, moat or swamp that squished underfoot. A wispy sway of cedars gave it an eerie feel. Reeds grew several feet high.

The sound of a child's crying drew her to a stream. Sobs rose from the water's depth. Ivory leaned at the edge, at soft, dark bubbles, and the crying stopped. She wondered how a child could have fallen and survived.

Bubbles cleared. Ivory found herself gazing at her own reflection. She saw it then: a face at the bottom of the pool returning her stare. A ripple, and the face was gone. Ivory peered into the black depths, seeking the mirage in the water.

Something touched her shoulder.

A water child stood there. But she was not a child. She was a woman fully grown and naked as Eve, save for an amulet and a string of olive leaves around her lower waist. She wore a teardrop face, jewel-bright eyes, skin beaded with water. She dazzled in the darkness. A soft blue fall of buttock-length hair caressed her back. She was petite and stunning even in melancholy. Air around her was encased in gloom. Her doom crept towards Ivory, who squinted, so dark was it.

Her fingers longed to touch that dense hair. Instead, she said: 'Dotto?' stunned at her own instinct.

'How do you know my name?' Dotto's whisper was as frail as it was old.

Seeing her firsthand, Ivory understood now the songs in the myth, the songs of her radiance. How her eyes told of diamonds, how her skin was soft as a riverbed, fresh as fruit, how her beauty reigned infinite. But of laughter that bubbled eager as thought, Ivory saw nothing.

'I am a friend,' she said to the river nymph.

'I have no friends.'

'What about Muntu?' said Ivory. 'Is he not a friend?'

'Harlequna! You must not speak that name.'

'Why not?'

'He is dead.' The montage of her beauty dimmed. Greys and shadows dulled it, an aura of dinginess.

'What if I said I can take you to him?'

Blue hair swung. 'My world is bleak, I have no patience. Did the ghost of my father send you to remind me of my torment?'

'But Muntu lives!'

'Harlequna!' Dotto's cry was a terrible sound that rolled in the wind. Its echo swayed in circular waves that compressed Ivory's hearing. 'Why must you goad me like this?'

Ivory's hand fell upon her shoulder.

'His spirit is alive. He asked me to give you this message: Close your eyes and think about the sea.'

And Dotto burst to new crying. 'I have never seen a sea. How can I think about one?'

'It is giant water that is green, and it is full of waves.' Ivory did not know why she said this.

But Dotto smiled. 'Like the waves that Great Chief Goanna parted and the waters swallowed the white man?'

Ivory smiled. 'Like those waters.'

Dotto pulled a reed from the ground. She put it to her lips like a flute and began to play. Her music was drama and destiny caught in tragedy. It rose and fell with yearning and purgatory. Tears cascaded down her face as she played. Wind caught and floated her hair. Now the instrument belted a tune of rage. Lightning. Thunder. A storm swelled in loops and pace, and when it crawled, the music also crawled and abruptly silenced.

Dotto slipped trembling to the ground and wept.

14.

How astonishing. The invisible barrier, so peculiar, it was one-way and particular. Dotto stepped through with no difficulty.

Watching her passage was like watching a shape on a distorting mirror, the kind of mirror you found in a carnival that changed how you saw yourself. It was reminiscent of the funhouse experience, many years ago, another memory with Sister Immaculata.

'It's the science of light,' the sister explained patiently, as the children giggled and pointed at their unexpected bodies. 'The mirrors are curved, and you get tall or short, depending on the tilt, where you are standing.'

Heaven knows where the young sister got the money for the fair, or how she managed to convince the cunning crow, Sister Hildegarde, that the children could do with an outing when they were not locked up or scrubbing floors. Sister Immaculata, bless her, she tried everything to stitch normality into the children's lives. But you never outdid the mother superior; you never truly did, no matter how you tried. You eventually came undone.

Now here was Ivory again, in a distorting mirror of sorts and this time it wasn't funny. She was anxious to reach Muntu, reunite him with Dotto.

As Dotto stepped through the barrier, she appeared to form and unform, weave and morph into misshapen bits that walked to the other side. First her foot, long and bendy, went through, pulling along a vertical half of her body, also malleable, across the threshold. A dancing elongated other foot followed and, finally, she was whole, perfect on the other side.

Going through herself, a few steps behind, Ivory didn't notice much difference – no change of temperature or surface, just a stepping.

They emerged in a sprawling full of trees that stood long and sleek. There was the big, green sky, the necklace of trees around a yellow hill.

'He was here,' said Ivory.

She looked around. Nothing. Muntu… he was nowhere in sight.

Dotto seemed to curl into herself. Ivory touched her arm lightly. 'He can't be far.' she said.

But Dotto shrugged the touch away. She was disintegrating, literally. She was thinning to nothing.

Suddenly he was there, as if out of the air.

Ivory saw him first. She noted that he had found cover for his nakedness.

He took in the scene. 'Dotto!'

Her fading halted. 'Muntu?' Her voice was small, coming and going like white noise in a broken transmission.

'Dotto.'

She started reforming.

'Muntu.' Her voice was a little stronger, no longer coming and going.

He thundered towards her in his hulking frame, norming to reasonable height as he approached. She became full once more. They collapsed into each other.

'Dotto.' He was sobbing.

'Harlequna!' she said, eyes soft in her tear-drop face. 'It really is you. All of you!'

He mulled it over, holding her as she trembled. 'Actually –'

A finger to his lip silenced him. 'Together. At last.' Diamond eyes sought onyx ones. 'Arm in arm in the stars.'

'Arm in arm in the stars,' he agreed.

'But –' she pulled from him. 'Something is different.'

He spoke to her hair. 'We *are* different.'

She cupped his face. 'There's something. About you.'

He closed his eyes. When he opened them, they were shadowed with more shadows.

He spoke, his voice distant. 'I am the shell of the man I used to be.'

'Is it the fire?'

Ivory explained. 'Muntu's twin souls separated when –'

'But I live,' he said. 'Death was a transition.'

'Yet you only live as a fraction,' Dotto said sadly. 'Where is he? The twin of your soul?'

And so Ivory told them of the buntu, and the destruction of its path, and how right now as they spoke, it was trapped inside the body of the man she loved and could kill him.

'Its path is lost, its thirst unquenchable. Re-unite, and all three of you will find peace. You must come to the place of dreams.'

Suddenly, she was filled with the same discerning spirit she had experienced when the amulet glowed a dazzling orange, and she pictured a meadow and found escape from Goth. Now, even without the amulet – and this knowledge surprised her the most – she felt the same discernment and knew what she must do. She also knew that she did not need Ginny to do it.

15.

Muntu found the mandisa cone and the cabbage palm.

Ivory led the chant: 'Oom-ba! Oom-ba!'

Dotto took up the dance and sang of a man who was the tallest, most beautiful being anyone had ever seen. And the proudest.

Muntu sat cross-legged on the ground, wrapped in smoke. He focused his energy on his twin, beckoning, pleading: 'Come home, my brother. Come home.'

'Oom-ba! Oom-ba!'

'Come home, my brother. Come home.'

In the deepest corner of the forest, at the border of two worlds, leaves began to tremble. A vicious wind, fast and loud, whirred around the three beings in the purging ceremony. The world spun. A force tore through Ivory and threw her to the ground. Someplace close, she heard Dotto's cry.

'Oom-ba! Oom-ba!' chanted Ivory.

'Come home, my brother. Come home.'

The amulet glowed like a beacon.

Muntu broke from the ground, arms spread like a messiah. He threw his head back, took a step forward. He began to run. A spear of ungodly flame shafted his way. He flew at speed, headed for the light. Stars at the horizon watched his race. Ivory felt the whip of wind on her face. She crawled to her knees, gasping with Dotto. They clawed toward each other and fell in a clasp. Breathless, they watched the collision.

The impact echoed far, tremors that shook the ground. Muntu fell and his cry was terrible to hear.

And the heat...

16.

... transported Ivory straight back to Earth.

She was on a bed, in a room, her room. Ginny Mo'unga lay next to her.

Ivory looked around at faces rugged with worry.

There was Bahati and Nick Hogan and Sam and Slobber – all peering at her, and then Slobber was licking her all over.

Beside her, the medicine woman stirred with a groan. Her woolly hair was still yellow as corn but now dishevelled and mostly flat.

'What happened?' Ivory croaked.

'I thought I had lost you.' Bahati stroked her forehead, beaded with sweat. 'One minute I was violently ill, about to explode cell by cell... And you! You appeared to have fainted. I got the phone to the bedside... And then Sam was here, and Ginny was here, and Nick was here. And Ginny was climbing on the bed beside you. Next thing I knew, both of you were having these awful tremors and you and Ginny went into a coma.'

Ivory smiled wanly. She looked at the people around her and she was moved. 'Are you all here for me? For us?' There was a sting of tears at the edge of her eyes. Her fingers sought Ginny, whose face carried much knowledge. 'How long were we gone?'

'Long enough.' Ginny unfurled from the bed.

'Seventeen minutes, Luscious.' It was Sam.

Ivory didn't rise to his bait, shoot him down with words. Instead she smiled, 'One-trick pony, huh? That flirting ever work anywhere?'

She glanced at Ginny, elusive yet present, wearing her robes and a voice older than Jacob, yet she was so young.

She thought of Mama Pebble and the meddlesome twins – would she see them again? They were her... *good* foster family. She thought of Muntu and Dotto and understood that the curse was gone. They would be fine. Muntu was a descendant of Great Chief Goanna, and so was Ivory. He was family. One day, alone, she would seek out the medicine woman and iron out some things. Questions of her past whose answers carried weight.

Ivory slid from the bed. 'Soda and rum anyone?' Grunts all around. 'That's a yes, then.'

Sam took her elbow but Bahati pushed him aside. 'Here, I'll take this one.'

She held onto him, Bahati, the man who was a cross between a geek and a feral, and he was hers. All her life Ivory had never possessed much, now she felt overwhelmed with abundance. 'Did you seriously survive a buntu?'

'Did you know…' strong hands around her waist. 'The name Bahati is of African origin – in Swahili it means a blessing.'

'Streuth. That's great.' Sam ran a hand through his hair. 'That's just great – is that how you get the girls?'

As for Nick…

He remained much bewildered. 'Seriously, mate, I tell you Whitey. I'm pretty dark on all this.'

'I know.' Ivory smiled.

Later she would tell him about the spiritual world Ginny had opened to her, about land that had elevated itself when an evil deed was done, about ancient terrain in the galaxy of independents, about the healing of Mama Pebble in a smoking that spread healing to Earth, about herself – how she had needed to discover herself and her own roots (she was still consolidating her identity), her newfound capabilities of a medium…

She caught Ginny's coal eyes.

The medicine woman's words burned in Ivory's head. *To follow the path of the seer, sacrifices must be made.*

After all I've been through, is that not sacrifice enough? asked Ivory with her mind.

Only you know what is sacrifice enough.

'Operation Limelight's solved, then, is it Whitey?' Nick's question interrupted her silent conversation with the seer.

'I believe it is.'

"How will you explain it all to Pugley?"

Superintendent Grant Pugley, cantankerous as ever. She had forgotten about him, she would be under fierce examination. But he had put together a budget that included a seer; surely he would understand. Would he, though? It took someone open to new ideas, to different ways of seeing the mundane world, to conjure up some semblance of understanding all this.

'Rum and I have to think about it for a minute. Or perhaps –' she looked at Nick. 'Perhaps you will explain it to Pugs.'

'Me? Why!'

'That's what happens when you call people Whitey.'

She reflected upon her past, and her gaze softened. Time did not heal old wounds – she had learnt to repair herself. Or perhaps it was the amulet that healed her. Well, it was back with its rightful owner, and she knew she no longer needed it. How did you repair yourself from choice? All her life there had been choices she did not make – someone made them for her. But Bahati… She looked at him. Bahati was her choice. He was her river, her mountain, her rock.

She smiled, a little sadly, and made another choice.

'But there's another reason,' she said.

All eyes fell on her. Her gaze refused to meet Bahati's.

'Look outside,' she said. 'See the mist?'

'There's no mist,' said Nick.

'It's there, right there, flowing like a network – calculating, unapologetic. And it's entered this room, our very veins, reshaping the way we see, how we feel, what we understand.'

The seer did not question this logic, nor did Bahati.

Sam said, 'The heck?'

Nick simply stared.

'I have unfinished business in Orange Crater.'

About the Author

Eugen Bacon is African Australian, a computer scientist mentally re-engineered into creative writing. Her work has won, been shortlisted, longlisted or commended in national and international awards, including the Bridport Prize, Copyright Agency Prize, Ron Hubbard's Writers of the Future Award, Australian Shadows Awards and Nommo Award for Speculative Fiction by Africans.

Eugen is a recipient of the Katharine Susannah Prichard (KSP) Emerging Writer-in-Residence 2020. Her creative work has appeared in literary and speculative fiction publications worldwide, including *Award Winning Australian Writing*, *Unsung Stories*, *Andromeda*, *Aurealis*, *Bards and Sages Quarterly*, *Meniscus*, *The Victorian Writer*, *Text Journal*, *Newswrite* – Writing NSW, British Science Fiction Association's *Vector Magazine* and through Routledge in *New Writing*. Recent publications: *Claiming T-Mo* (Meerkat Press), Writing Speculative Fiction (Macmillan). In 2020: *Her Bitch Dress* (Ginninderra Press) *The Road to Woop Woop & Other Stories* (Meerkat Press), *Hadithi* (Luna Press); *Ivory's Story* (NewCon Press).

Author's Acknowledgements

To Dominique Hecq for your scholarly knowledge and advice, your generosity and encouragement, in places of within, without. The hybrids we are.

To publisher Ian Whates of *NewCon Press* for seeing, truly seeing, this fiction that is literary and cultural. A speculative tale that is a mystery and a history. An origins story about finding who you are.

Also from NewCon Press

London Centric – Edited by Ian Whates

Future Tales of London. **Neal Asher, Mike Carey, Geoff Ryman, Aliette de Bodard, Dave Hutchinson, Aliya Whiteley, Eugen Bacon** and more. Militant A.I.s, virtual realities, augmented realities and alternative realities; a city where murderers stalk the streets, where drug lords rule from the shadows, and where large sections of the population are locked in time stasis, but where tea is still sipped in cafés on the corner and the past still resonates with the future...

Lockdown Tales –Neal Asher

Best-selling author Neal Asher was far from idle during lockdown, keeping busy in the best way possible: he wrote. Five brand new novellas and novelettes and one novella reworked and expanded from a story first published in 2019. Together, they form Lockdown Tales, exploring the Polity universe and beyond. What lies in wait for humanity after the Polity has gone? Six stories, 150,000 words of fiction that crackle with energy, invention and excitement.

Dark Harvest – Cat Sparks

Award-winning author Cat Sparks writes science fiction with a distinct Australian flavour – stories steeped in the desperate anarchy of Mad Max futures, redolent with scorching sun and the harshness of desert sands, but her narratives reach deeper than that. In her tales of ordinary people adapting to post-apocalyptic futures, she casts a light on what it means to be human; the good and the bad, the noble and the shameful.

Frequencies of Existence – Andrew Hook

Andrew Hook sees the world through a different lens. He takes often mundane things and coaxes the reader to find strangeness, beauty, and horror in their form; he colours the world in surreal shades and leads the reader down discomforting paths where nothing is quite as it should be. *Frequencies of Existence* features twenty-four of his finest stories, including four that are original to this collection.